KALEIDOSCOPE
EYES

KALEIDOSCOPE EYES

JEN BRYANT

ALFRED A. KNOPF
New York

THIS IS A BORZOI BOOK PUBLISHED BY ALFRED A. KNOPF

All rights reserved. Published in the United States by Alfred A. Knopf, an imprint of Random House Children's Books, a division of Random House, Inc., New York.

Knopf, Borzoi Books, and the colophon are registered trademarks of Random House, Inc.

Visit us on the Web! www.randomhouse.com/kids

Educators and librarians, for a variety of teaching tools, visit us at www.randomhouse.com/teachers

Library of Congress Cataloging-in-Publication Data
Bryant, Jennifer.
Kaleidoscope eyes / Jen Bryant. — 1st ed.
    p.   cm.
Summary: In 1968, while the Vietnam War rages, thirteen-year-old Lyza inherits a project from her deceased grandfather, who was using his knowledge of maps and the geography of Lyza's New Jersey hometown to locate the lost treasure of Captain Kidd.
ISBN 978-0-375-84048-7 (trade) — ISBN 978-0-375-94048-4 (lib. bdg.) — ISBN 978-0-375-85365-4 (e-book)
[1. Novels in verse. 2. Maps—Fiction. 3. Research—Fiction. 4. Buried treasure—Fiction. 5. Single-parent families—Fiction. 6. Vietnam War, 1961–1975—Fiction. 7. Family life—New Jersey—Fiction. 8. New Jersey—History—20th century—Fiction. 9. Mystery and detective stories.] I. Title.
PZ7.5.B792Kal 2009
[Fic]—dc22
2008027345

Printed in the United States of America
May 2009
10 9 8 7 6 5 4 3
First Edition

Now and then we had a hope
that if we lived and were good,
God would permit us to be pirates.

—from *Life on the Mississippi*
by Mark Twain (1835–1910),
American writer and humorist

For Neil

Part I

Quietly turning the back door key,
Stepping outside, she is free.

—from "She's Leaving Home"

by John Lennon and Paul McCartney

KARMA

I wake up every morning
to Janis Joplin.

My sister, Denise, has a life-size poster of Janis—
mouth open in a scream around the microphone,
arms raised, hair frizzed out wildly,
an anguished, contorted look on her face—
thumbtacked right above her desk,
which is directly across the hall from my bed
and one hundred percent dead ahead
in my direct line of sight.
Janis is the first thing I see when I return from sleep
and reenter reality.

In a normal house, the simple answer to this would be:
close the door. But I do not live
in a normal house. I live in a tumble-
down, three-story, clapboard Victorian
where the rooms get smaller as you climb the stairs,
mine being barely larger than a closet and having—
like all the other rooms on the third floor—

no door (Dad says the former owners, who went broke,
used them for firewood before they moved),
across the hall from my sister, who's nineteen
and who believes anyway
that walls and doors "interrupt the flow" of her karma,
and so of course this leaves me no choice
in the matter of Janis.

When I pointed out to Denise
that my future mental health was probably in jeopardy
because of it, she just sneered and said:
"Get over it, Lyza—you're already a Bradley,
so mental health
is out of the question for you anyway."

Whoever said "the baby of the family
gets all the sympathy"
was clearly *not*
the baby.

JUNE 1, 1966

It's been almost two years since that day,
when our family began to unravel
like a tightly wound ball of string
that some invisible tomcat
took to pawing and flicking across the floor,
pouncing upon it again and again,
so those strands just kept loosening
and breaking   apart
until all we had left was a bunch of frayed,
chewed-up bits
scattered all over the house.

Mom had left twice before,
after she and Dad had a fight
over money. She stayed away overnight,
but both times she came back, acting like
nothing had happened. This time, the three of us thought,
would be the same . . . it just might take
a little longer.

Days became weeks. I finished sixth grade.
Dad, who already taught math full-time
at Glassboro State, started to teach at night.
We almost never saw him.
Denise tore up her college applications,
got hired as a waitress at the Willowbank Diner,
started sneaking around with Harry Keating
and his hippie crowd.

Still, we hoped Mom would come back.
For the entire summer,
Dad left the porch light on
and the garage door unlocked every evening
around the same time
Mom used to come home
from her art-gallery job in Pleasantville.

I'd lie awake until real late,
wondering where she could be,
if she was OK, if she might be
hurt, lost, or sick.

Denise sent letters through Mom's best friend,
Mrs. Corman, the only one who knew
where Mom had gone.
Mom answered them at first, but she never
gave a return address. Then, for no reason,
her letters to Denise and to Mrs. Corman
stopped.

Even so, I had hope.
Every evening, I set her place
at the dinner table and bought candy
on her birthday, just in case.

When September came, I started seventh grade.
I kept my report cards and vaccination records

in the family scrapbook
so that when she came back, she could pick up
mothering
right where she'd left off.

Long after Dad and Denise
had made their peace
with the reality of our broken family, I still believed
Mom would come home.
I believed the way I had once believed
in Santa Claus and the Easter Bunny.

Then one day last year, I was
walking home from Willowbank Junior High
when I noticed the library flag
flying at half-mast,
so I asked
Mrs. Leinberger, our town librarian,
why.

"Charley Prichett, Guy Smith, and Edward Cullinan
were killed in Vietnam," she said.

I knew them all—
their families lived on our end of town.
Charley, Eddie, and Guy
had graduated from Willowbank High
with Denise.
Mrs. Leinberger put her hand

on my shoulder. "They're not coming back
to Willowbank, Lyza—I'm sorry. . . ."

Not coming back. . . . Not coming back. . . .

Her words thrummed against the inside
of my head
like the machine guns I'd seen and heard
on the evening news.

Not coming back. . . . Not coming back. . . .

Like the blades of choppers
lifting half-dead men
from the swamps and jungles,
the phrase sliced through any shred
of hope I had left.

That night, I threw the scrapbook
in the trash,
set the dinner table for three,
and gave Denise
a large heart-shaped box of chocolates,
which she took down to the record store
to share with Harry
and the rest of their hippie friends.

KALEIDOSCOPE EYES

Some nights, before I go to sleep,
I look through the lens of the
one Mom gave me

for my tenth birthday, just to see how, when I
turn the tube slowly around,
every fractured pattern that bends and splits

into a million little pieces
always comes back together, to make a picture
more beautiful than the one before.

MALCOLM DUPREE

He's thirteen
—like me.

He lives in a three-story clapboard Victorian
on Gary Street
—like me.

He's an eighth grader
at Willowbank Junior High
—like me.

He's in Mrs. Smithson's homeroom,
Mr. Bellamy's Earth Science,
and Mr. Hogan's Math
—like me.

He roots for the Phillies
—like me.

He's the younger of two kids
in his family (but his brother, Dixon, is
a LOT nicer than Denise)
—like me.

You see, Malcolm and me,
we've been friends since we were little,
since the day I finally got tired of trying to tag along
with Denise and her girlfriends.
That afternoon, according to Dad, I looked out
the window and saw Malcolm playing in the street.
I went outside, told him my name, then rode
my tricycle down the block to his house,
where we played every outdoor kids' game
we could think of:

Cops and Robbers

Red Light, Green Light

Jump rope

Hide-and-Seek

        Dodgeball   Hopscotch

until it was time for supper and my father
came to take me home.
"You'd never thrown a tantrum,
but that night you and Malcolm hid
                      under the Duprees' front porch,
where none of us could squeeze in
and reach you. You refused to come out unless we promised
you could play again the whole *next* day, just the same.
Of course we promised . . . and ever since,
you two have gotten along
like peas in a pod."

UNWRITTEN RULES

You'd think
with a beginning like that,
and with all those things in common,
that Malcolm and me would spend a lot of time together
at school.

But we don't.

We sure didn't make the rules
about who can be friends with whom,
and we don't *like* the rules the way they are . . .
but we are also not fools.

There are three hundred other kids in our school
and as far as I can tell, not one of them has
a best friend
who's a different color.

And so—
in the halls, at lunch, and in class,
Malcolm stays with the other black kids
and I stay with the other white kids
and most of the time
it isn't until we leave the building at 3:05
that we even say hi.

ON THE OTHER HAND . . .

there's my *other* best friend, Carolann Mott,
who lives across the street

with her mother, father, and younger twin brothers—
Scott and Pete—
whom I still can't tell apart
even after five years of trying.

Anyway . . . aside from the color of their skin
and the fact that Malcolm's a guy
and Carolann's a girl,
my two best friends could not possibly be
more different.

Malcolm is the quiet, thoughtful type . . . careful
about everything he does. If he were a bird,
he'd be one of those great blue herons
that we often see at the edge of the river,
wading cautiously on long, skinny legs,
planning his every step.

Carolann, on the other hand,
is more like those sandpipers
you see at the beach:
small and quick, always on the move,
checking out the surf, then scampering back.
Carolann hardly ever sits still—unless
she's snacking or reading one of her mystery books:
    The Scarlet Slipper Mystery
    The Phantom of Pine Hill
    The Secret of the Golden Pavilion
Someday, she wants to be a private investigator.

After Carolann's family moved here six years ago,
it took a while for her and Malcolm
to trust each other.
Malcolm said she was nosy (she *does* love to gossip);
Carolann said Malcolm was a snob.
"He's just quiet around kids
he doesn't know," I told her. But they stayed
apart.

Then one night when our family was
at the movies in Williamstown, there was a bad
storm. Two big trees and some electrical wires came
down on top of the Motts' roof. Malcolm's dad
was the first one on their doorstep,
offering to help. The Motts had to get out,
but they didn't want to
                                    split up   their family.
Mr. Dupree, who's the pastor at Willowbank A.M.E.,
asked his parishioners to set up
blankets and cots on the second floor,
and he let Carolann's family live there
in the church for two weeks. Mrs. Dupree brought them food.
After school, Malcolm and Dixon entertained the twins
so Carolann's parents could meet with the insurance men
and supervise repairs.

Ever since then,
Malcolm and Carolann have been

almost as good friends as Malcolm and me.
Especially in the summer, when we don't have to worry
about school or who
sits with whom at lunch or in class,
the three of us are often together.
And whenever I'm with Carolann and Malcolm
at the same time, I become
the monkey   in the middle   between
a tall, shy black guy and a small, hyperactive white girl
and that's when *I* feel
almost normal.

1968

So far,
this year's not been so great.

In January,
the North Vietnamese came by the thousands
out of the jungles
and into the cities
and attacked our embassy.

In February,
Walter Cronkite went on TV
and told everyone
that what was actually happening in Vietnam
and what our government
was telling us was happening in Vietnam
were two entirely different things.

In March,
at a Tennessee rally for peace and civil rights,
sixty people got hurt,
lots more got arrested,
and one sixteen-year-old boy
was killed.

In April,
Dr. Martin Luther King, Jr., was murdered
by a hidden assassin
at a hotel in Memphis.
Malcolm's mom cried for two days straight.
Malcolm stayed locked in his room
and didn't come out
till after the funeral (they showed it on TV)
was over.

In May,
in Paris, France,
students took to the streets

to protest their government,
and nine million French workers
went on strike.

Soon it will be June,
and as we close the textbooks, take out the lawn mowers
and wicker chairs,
everyone here in Willowbank, New Jersey,
is desperate
for signs of improvement.

BEACHES, PEACHES, CARS

"Like ants to a picnic," Dad loves to say.
And that really *is* how it looks
every summer Saturday
as families in cars on their way to the beach
form an endless stream—the entire length of Main Street—
smack through the center of town.

When Mom was still here, when Denise and I
were little, we used to go to the beach
almost every weekend . . .
stay to swim and play for the whole day,

buy tomatoes and fresh peaches at the farm stands
on the way home,
be back in Willowbank by dark. But the last time
we went as a family,
Mom and Dad had a big fight.
We left the beach early, didn't stop for peaches
or tomatoes or even ice cream.
We were home by midafternoon.

Wildwood, my favorite beach, is less than an hour away
from Willowbank . . .
but I haven't been there since that day.

Instead, starting on weekends in late May,
I've taken to sitting on the bench
before Miller's grocery store,
watching those same cars going home. I stare into each
and every backseat
until I see a face that looks sad or angry or both,
till I get my proof
that having a regular family and time to spend with them
doesn't necessarily make you
happy.

EUPHORIA

Denise is scribbling this word
on her calendar
in the box for July twenty-second.

I don't know what it means.

It sounds like the name
of some Greek or Roman queen,
or like one of those countries in Asia
that I can never remember on my geography tests.

I ask Denise, but she pretends she doesn't hear me
and sings loudly along with "People Got to Be Free,"
which is playing on WABC,
while she gets dressed
in the layers of gauze she calls a shirt,
a too-long macramé belt, and a skirt
that's so short
you could mistake it for a headband.

Tonight she's meeting Harry Keating
and a bunch of his friends
so they can plan
a peace rally with the students in Princeton.
(*That* I'd like to see . . . the young geniuses of America
taking orders from Denise
and a bunch of amateur disk jockeys.)

When she leaves, I find Mom's old dictionary
and look up *euphoria*.
It says: "rapture," "ecstasy," "joy,"
which can only mean one of two things:
a. Denise plans to leave us that day and join some flower-child
   commune.
b. Blues goddess Janis is performing somewhere near us.

Sadly, my money's on Janis.

Part 2

**Freedom's just another word for nothin'
left to lose.**

—from "Me and Bobby McGee"

music and lyrics by Kris Kristofferson and Fred Foster

sung by Janis Joplin

BLACK IS NOT MY BEST COLOR

When we get the phone call, I go right
to the hall closet, turn on the light.

The black dress I've worn to every funeral
so far these past two years
still hangs there next to
Denise's Grim Reaper Halloween costume,
which—considering all of our recent losses—
I'm beginning to think
might be more appropriate.

First there was Carolann's cousin Tom,
shot down in Vietnam,
then Charley, Eddie, and Guy—
Denise's friends from Willowbank High
(also killed in action)—
then our neighbor Mr. Metzger's daughter,
overdosed at a rock concert.
And I guess I should count my mother
(who is hopefully *not* dead, but might as well be
for all we see of her).

Now Gramps is gone, too. His heart,
which had quit on him once before,
finally gave out.

Lately, I've been to so many funerals, I feel like
I can recite the preacher's part
almost word for word,
and I have my phrases of sympathy for the family
so well practiced, I hardly
have to plan them anymore.

This time, though, Dad, Denise, and me
will be the grievers
and all our neighbors and friends in Willowbank
will be the sympathy-givers
and as I pull that plain black dress from the closet,
smooth the wrinkles,
check the buttons and the hem,
I am wondering what, exactly,
I should say back to them.

GRAMPS

As a young man, my father's father
joined the Navy
so he could see the world.

As it turns out, he *did* see most of it—
"I have set foot on every continent, Lyza,"
he used to tell me. "Except Antarctica,
which I don't particularly need to see . . .
and I have traversed every ocean at least once—
most of them several times."

When the Navy found out he was good at math,
they made Gramps a navigator,
put him in charge of all the maps and charts
on the ship. Even when he left the Navy,
he could not give them up.
Whenever we visited him in Tuckahoe, New Jersey,
where he and Grandma had lived for fifty years
and where they'd raised my father,
he'd be poring over his *Rand-McNally World Atlas*
or a set of sailing charts and maps,
balanced carefully on his lap.

And Dad, who inherited his father's knack
for math but who is, in my opinion, allergic to risk,
would shake his head. "Pop, you'll always be
a sailor," he'd say before leaving the room
to find something more practical to do.

But I would always stay.
Gramps would take my hand, lead me
up to the attic, where he'd roll out across the table
a map of the South Pacific
or a nautical chart of the Caribbean Sea.

"Where shall we sail today, Lyza?" he'd ask,
and I'd reply, "Australia!" or "Jamaica!"
and, using a compass and a ruler,
we'd plot our course across the waters,
just me and him together,
a real adventure.

Once, Gramps showed me photos of when,
years earlier, he'd tried to sail
alone
from Florida to Maine,
with just his maps, a compass, a radio, and a two-week
supply of water and food.

He didn't make it. The Coast Guard rescued him,
a big storm having blown his boat
onto the rocks of the Massachusetts coast.
"Weren't you scared?" I asked him.
"Terrified—almost the whole time," Gramps answered.
"But," he added, "I'd never felt more alive."

"Darn fool . . . nearly killed himself" was how
Dad explained it later on the drive
back to Willowbank.

So that's how it was when we'd visit: the rest of them
downstairs
playing cards, making cookies, or watching TV;

me and Gramps in the attic,
sailing around the world.

But then Denise and I got older,
and Mom and Dad were fighting all the time.
We visited Gramps and Grandma
less and less . . . it was too hard, I guess.

Just once more, after Grandma died, we stood
all together on the shore
while Gramps scattered her ashes
in the waves.

Now Gramps is gone.
Mom, wherever she is, probably doesn't know,
which isn't fair to us, or to Gramps, who always treated her
like a daughter—
but of course since we have
no address, no telephone number, not even
a city or a state or a *country*
where we can try and find her,
there *is* no way to tell her, and that really stinks.

Anyway . . . Dad has decided that Gramps should be buried
in Willowbank Cemetery,
overlooking the Mullica River,
which flows slowly through South Jersey
before it empties into the sea.

WHEN IT RAINS, IT POURS

Before Dad left for work,
he took a walk around the block—
four times.
I'm pretty sure I saw him crying.

Yesterday, in California,
Bobby Kennedy won the Democratic primary election.
Then he got shot
and died.

QUIET AS A MOUSE

The night after Gramps' funeral, I can't sleep.
I lie on my side
and point my kaleidoscope toward the streetlights;
that kills ten minutes.

I count sheep, dogs, and cats. Still awake. I think
about Mom: if she'd
known about Gramps' funeral, would she have come?
Maybe; maybe

not. (Maybe I should give up trying to figure her out.)
I go down-

stairs, drink a couple of Coca-Colas,
and watch

a rerun of *The Ed Sullivan Show* without the sound.
Today at the cemetery,
I didn't cry much; but when Ed's mouse puppet,
Topo Gigio,

appears in his little red and white nightie
and his cap
and kisses "Eddie" on the cheek, I start blubbering
like a baby.

Gramps used to love watching that part
of the show.
Back in bed, I lie awake just thinking, but then
my mind gets

interrupted by my bladder and I have to get up
and walk
down the hall to the bathroom.
On my way

back the last time, I spot something moving
in the yard:
it's Harry Keating, tossing pebbles at
Denise's window.

I hear her lift the sash, see her climb out onto
the half-roof

that covers our back door. Harry climbs up
the fire escape,

and the two of them sit there laughing, smoking,
and kissing
while my father sleeps in total ignorance
one floor below.

I stand at the small hall window awhile
and, for some
strange reason that I can't explain, my natural
urge to

disturb them, make some noise, expose their
secret meeting,
for some strange reason that usual feeling
vanishes.

Instead, for a few brief seconds, I actually
admire Denise—
despite her annoying habits and her belief
that Janis Joplin

is one step down from God, she's always ready
to take a chance,
just like Gramps. Maybe Mom felt that way, too.
Maybe that's why

living in Willowbank just wasn't quite
enough.

ALTERED IMAGE

On Tuesday, when Denise slept over
at her friend Suzi's place, I taped my blown-up photo
of the North Wildwood Beach
over Janis's face.

You could still see the rest of her sticking out
underneath, but at least
I woke up to sand and surf and sun
instead of a screaming freak.

I could almost feel my brain cells regenerating.

Denise threw a fit when she came home.
She tore my photo
down,
tossed it onto my bed. "God, Lyza. You're so square. . . .
You should have been born two hundred years ago—
Janis is *so way past you!*"

I replied that would be just fine—
I'd love to live in a time
when parents of teenage girls had the right
to shoot any unwanted suitors they found slinking around
the house at night.

That shut her up for a while.

TUCKAHOE

I don't want to go.
Neither does Denise. It's too soon. Too sad.
We both make excuses:

Denise: "Dad, I can't . . . have to work double shift
        at the diner. They're short of help for the weekend."

Me: "I promised I'd spend Saturday at the library with
        Carolann. We have to study for history,
        then we're going to the movies."

Dad sighs. His solution to raising two teenage daughters
alone
is to keep a full refrigerator
and teach as many college classes as possible
so he never has to be home.
He is not—has never been—
one for family conversations, *or* for handing out
discipline.

He runs his hand through his thick,
rapidly graying hair.
He looks at us both, square.
He speaks quietly, but firmly:
"Denise. Lyza. On Saturday morning I will be
in the car, out front, at exactly seven. I expect
both of you

to be already sitting in the backseat. I expect
you will come with me to Gramps' place,
to help do
whatever needs doing, together,
and I expect it will take
most of the day."

Dad stands up, walks away.
Denise and I sit there awhile, a little stunned
that our father,
who usually reserves most of his words
for his college students, has actually
spoken quite a few of them
to us.

DIARY OF A SATURDAY MORNING

6:40 Alarm rings. Get up. Wake Denise.

6:45 Brush teeth. Comb hair. Wake Denise.

6:50 Put on blue jeans, T-shirt, sandals. Wake Denise.

6:55 Pinch Denise's foot. Run.

6:59 Slide into backseat of Dad's Chevy; he's already behind the wheel.

7:00 Wait for Denise.

7:05 Dad, between clenched teeth: "Lyza, *please* go inside and get your sister. . . ."

7:09 Leave Willowbank. Denise, braless and shoeless, grumbling.

8:00 Arrive at Gramps' place in Tuckahoe.

8:05 Wander around the house. Wait for appraiser.

8:40 The appraiser, Mr. Brewster (three-piece suit; fat), arrives.

8:45–10:15 Dad walks through the house with Brewster. I nap in Gramps' backyard hammock. Denise flirts, quite successfully, with the neighbor's teenage son.

10:30 Watch Dad sign forms allowing Brewster to sell everything at public auction in mid-July.

10:45 Find an unopened jar of peanut butter and a package of saltines in the pantry, which I share with Dad and Denise. We eat in silence on the porch. Seagulls circle overhead, chattering. I think of Carolann.

11:00 Dad gives us each a large box, assigns us to different parts of the house. "Take whatever you want," he says, "for yourselves or for your children." (*Children?! Is he kidding?* Apparently not. . . .)

11:05 Dad leaves to check out the garage and toolshed. I suggest a trade with Denise: Grandma's closet for the attic. She agrees.

11:10–12:00 Go through the kitchen and small hallway downstairs. I take a set of silverware and four unbroken plates (we can use them now, back at our place). Clean out the pantry, wipe the shelves. Wrap Grandma's rosebud vase and a photo of her and Gramps in a linen napkin, place them carefully in my box.

12:05 Climb the steep, winding stairs to the third floor. The door is warped shut. I put down my box, throw my weight against the wood. It opens. I walk in.

ATTIC

Reaching up, I pull the chain to snap on
the one bare bulb hanging
from the low ceiling.

It looks and smells just like I remember:
the piles of books, the stacks of maps,
the long, slightly slanted table—

all just like I remember. I walk over to the chair
and sit where he sat so many times
with me on his lap.

I run my right hand slowly over the world map
he still has spread out,
and as it glides to the side it hits

the edge of a thick brown envelope,
which says, in Gramps' unmistakable, neat script:
FOR LYZA ONLY.

I'VE HAD ENOUGH SURPRISES LATELY

. . . thank you very much.
First Mom takes off with no explanation.
Then my older sister (who's a total pain,
but a pretty smart total pain who had plans for medical school)
barely graduates and decides
she'd rather wait tables and hang out
with Hairy Harry Keating,
who—as far as I can tell—
spends most of his time painting
posters to protest the war.

Then some of our neighbors come
back from Vietnam in coffins. Now my gramps is
gone and I didn't even get to say good-bye.
No wonder I'm starting to get
an uneasy, queasy feeling
whenever I face something (like this envelope)
that I don't expect. I sit stone-still a minute,
thinking about what might be in it:
Money? A diary from his Navy days? Pictures of
his solo sailing trip?

I sit there a long time,
wondering . . . thinking . . .
fingering the flap of the envelope.

CONTENTS UNDER PRESSURE

Finally, I work up the courage to open it.
Inside, there are three maps, carefully folded
and stacked, bound together by a single
rubber band. On top is this note:

> Dear Lyza,
>
> Here is a little project I started a while back,
> which I'm leaving for you to finish. It has kept
> me going these last few years, when my eyes were
> dimming, when my body was failing, when I
> sensed my time here was nearly spent. But
> please don't feel bad about any of that . . . it's just
> what happens. I have lived a good long life.
>
> They say we should grow "older and wiser" . . .
> mostly I just feel old. However, I do believe I've
> learned one thing: every life should have some
> risk. Among the hardships, disappointments,
> and losses, it's the adventure of it all that has
> gotten me up each morning. I know you and I
> are alike in this way. Your father, whom I love
> very much, prefers certainty, so he never
> understood me. Your sister is smart, but she
> never showed the interest in maps and charts
> that you did, even when you were little. That's
> why I've decided to leave this with you, and only

with you. Later, if there's a right time to share it,
I'm sure you'll know.

I'm sorry we won't have a chance to sail around
the world together. I would have enjoyed that.
I think you would have, too. I'm sorry I won't
have time to say good-bye. (I thought about
driving to Willowbank for one last visit, but
then ... well ... I decided I'd rather have you
remember me in happier, healthier days.) If you
choose to complete this project, I'll be with you,
in spirit, every step of the way.

With all my love,
Gramps

MAPS

Like I said, there are three of them
in a stack.
I click on the brass reading lamp above me,
clear a space
on the table, unfold Map Number One:

a complete
street map of the town of Willowbank
with three
places marked A, B, C in red pen, but
no description
to tell me what the three letters mean.
I wonder
if Gramps wanted to move closer to us
and maybe
he was looking at houses in our town.
But when I
look again, I see that the letters don't mark
homes:
A is in the elementary school yard, B is
in the park,
and C is in the woods behind the Willowbank
A.M.E. Church
(Malcolm says it stands for *African Methodist
Episcopal*),
where Mr. Dupree preaches on Sundays.
I fold up
the first map, take out Map Number Two,
which is smaller
and looks like a blueprint of the
Mullica River,
dated 1968, signed by some company
of land surveyors
and stamped with an official New Jersey
State seal.

Maybe Gramps was planning a last
solo trip
in his little sailboat down our own lazy
river,
just like Tom Sawyer and Huck Finn did
with their raft
on the Mississippi. This also makes me want
to cry, but I
try not to so I don't smudge the blueprint.
I fold over
Number Two and when I open Number Three,
I see there's
some sort of letter stapled to the upper
left-hand corner.

FROM THE FIRM

The letter says:

April 25, 1968

Dear Mr. Bradley:

I received your letter and the maps in question
on March 15. Thank you for sending them
to my attention. Since then, I have checked your
documents against several reliable sources
in our company's possession, as well as with
the archives of the State Geological Survey.

The result, I am pleased to inform you, is that
I find your calculations on the shift in course
of the Mullica River, and in particular as it pertains
to the section that now runs west of the town
of Willowbank, to be entirely correct.
I hope I have been of some good assistance.

Fee for research and calculations = $75—
payable by check, due in thirty days.

Sincerely,
John McGraw
John McGraw, civil engineer
Everhardt, McGraw, and Weibner Associates

NUMBER THREE

This one puzzles me.
It's also a map—but more like a picture,
drawn by hand and stamped
with the initials *L.B.*
in one of the lower corners.

At the top, it says "Mullica River—
approximation of its location in 1699."

In the other lower corner is the signature
of the engineer, John McGraw,
who wrote the letter
back to Gramps
about checking his maps and facts.

I look at the date again: *1699.*
Why would Gramps be interested
in where the Mullica River ran
way back then—which was even way *before*
Tom Sawyer and Huckleberry Finn?

I hear Denise's big bare feet slapping up the stairs.
I quick stack the maps back together,
stuff them inside the envelope,
which I turn
over this time. I see then that I've missed
one thing that is noted on the flip

side, in Gramps' precise handwriting:
    Brigantine Historical Society:
    File 276, drawer 11, document 7
and below that is a brass key
taped to the paper.

I place the envelope
and all of its contents in the box
beneath the photo of Grandma and Gramps,
the plates, and the rosebud vase,
where I know it will be safe from Denise's prying eyes,
since she has no interest in anything
she can't smoke, wear, or sing.

Part 3

Many's the time I've been mistaken
And many times confused.

—from "American Tune"

by Paul Simon

GUESSWORK

Now I'm just plain frustrated. Our visit to Tuckahoe
    was two whole weeks ago and every night since,
        when Dad and Denise are at work and Carolann

has to entertain the twins so her mother can clean up
    after dinner, I climb the stairs, empty the brown
        envelope, spread out everything on my desk

and all across my bedroom floor, and try to
    make sense of it. So far, here's what I've got:
        As a Navy navigator, my grandfather

planned routes for ships to travel across the seas
    and open oceans. OK, I get that. But then, for some
        strange reason, he got very interested in the Mullica—

not an ocean, but our very own South Jersey river,
    the one that flows just west of town,
        the one his gravestone looks over.

Try as I might, I can't reason it out. Maybe Gramps
    was getting senile. Maybe he just made up
        some wild plan for a solo voyage along the river

as a way to escape, kind of like we used to do
    together when I'd visit. But then—what about his
        hand-drawn map of the Mullica in 1699?

I did figure out *one* thing: "L.B." is most probably
    himself, Lewis Bradley. Anyway, that map is drawn
        on thin paper—almost like onionskin, almost like

it was supposed to be see-through. (Ha! Maybe Denise
    can use it for a shirt.) So, OK . . . I lay it on top of
        the map of the river labeled *1968*, and I see

right away it shows that how the river flows *now*
    is *not* the same as how the river flowed back then.
        I look through my kaleidoscope awhile

to clear my mind. Then I read over again that one
    part of the engineer's letter: "I find your calculations
        on the shift in course of the Mullica River, and in particular

as it pertains to the section that now runs west of the town
    of Willowbank, to be entirely correct." I didn't know
        a river could shift; I wonder, is this guy McGraw for real?

Or is he simply trying to get some fast cash from a
    tired old sailor? I lie on my back and stare at the
        cracks in the ceiling, branching off in a dozen

separate directions like little streams flowing from
    a larger body of water. "Tributaries" is what
        Mr. Bellamy called them last week when he

reviewed some terms for our Earth Science test,
    (which I barely passed, even though I actually
        studied this time). Only six days of eighth grade left.

Too bad—just when I'm finding a use for geology.

JUST CHECKING...

"Can a river shift?"
I blurt out at the end of science class,
after the bell has rung,
after everyone else has left.

Mr. Bellamy looks at me like I have
two heads. I don't blame him.
All year, I've only asked two other questions
in his class: "Can I please use the bathroom pass?"
and "Can I do some extra credit
to raise my D-minus?"

When he's shaken off his shock, he says:
"Well, yes . . . if you mean, Lyza,
can a river change its course over time—
then yes, absolutely, it most certainly can!"
He seems pleased to see that I'm at last
showing an interest in his class,
even if it *is* a little late.

He looks at me curiously. "Why do you ask?"
I hesitate. "Well . . .
I was reading something at my gramps' place . . ."
(which is true)
"and it made me wonder . . ."
I don't say it was a hand-drawn map
of the Mullica River in 1699. He might get
curious
and I'm not ready yet to let
anyone else know about this, especially a teacher.
So . . . I just let him think it was an atlas,
something normal like that.

Mr. Bellamy buys it.
He shifts into full-throttle teacher mode:
    "The earth, Lyza, is in a constant state of change. . . ."
    (waves hands excitedly)
    "The atmosphere, bodies of water, and tectonic plates
    are constantly interacting
    (weaves fingers together to demonstrate)

to re-create the geography we see around us. . . ."
(spreads arms out wide as if those plates
and bodies were right inside his classroom)

He has other things to say about
the earth, and he says most of them in the next
twenty minutes.

I try to listen, but I already have what I need:
a second opinion on the question
of shifting rivers,
which seems now to be a lot more
fact than fiction.

INDECISION

I "X" through another box on the calendar.
Another whole week has passed, school's out,
and I'm still no further along in the mystery of Gramps' maps
than I was before.

Except . . . I know a river can

shift,

and that my former-navigator grandfather
felt he needed to draw a map
of how the Mullica River flowed in 1699,
and to pay some engineer guy to verify
that he drew it right.

But I don't know *why* I need to know that.
So what's the use?

Then there's the key—
which doesn't seem to belong to anything
either here or back in Tuckahoe
(I checked before we left; it didn't fit any
of Gramps' doors or kitchen cabinets,
the garden shed, or the garage).

Then there's that note on the back of the envelope
about some document and file
at the Brigantine Historical Society.
But I don't have a license or a car . . . so how can I
get there and still keep this a secret
from Denise and Dad, which I assume is what Gramps
wanted me to do, or why else
would he have addressed the envelope
just to me?

"FOR LYZA *ONLY*" is the part that bothers me,
the part I've been thinking a lot *more* about lately

because his letter *also* said:
If there's a right time to share it, I'm sure you'll know.

So . . . is tonight the right time?

GOOD ADVICE

"Adventures are better together," Gramps used to say
whenever we planned a journey in the attic.
"Plus if you get into trouble, there's always
someone near
to lend a hand, save you from going under
when the current's too strong, when the seas get rough."

I take my kaleidoscope off the shelf,
where I've kept it ever since Mom left.
Funny—coming from her, it was the perfect gift:
colorful, like she always was;
slim, which is how I remember her;
and mostly . . . unpredictable.

I turn the cylinders
   around and
      around and
         around until I find a brand-new pattern,

in hopes that my brain
might catch on and do the same.
I put the kaleidoscope
aside,   look at the maps again.

Well, *that* doesn't work.

OK, I need to face it: I am either too dumb or too chicken
to figure out this map thing
alone.

I roll off my bed, slide down the banister,
pick up the hallway phone.
I dial Malcolm's number. He's home.
"Be over in ten," he says loud enough
to be heard over
his dad's Louis Armstrong records.

I go into the living room, lift
the front window, yell across to Carolann,
who's teaching the twins
how to play Mother, may I?

She waves when she hears me, picks them up—
one twin under each arm—
and carries them inside. She reappears on the porch steps
with three bottles of soda
and a big bag of Wise potato chips.

You know, I may not be able
to count on my family,
but my friends, at least, are as steady as they come.

NEVER TOO OLD FOR SHOW 'N' TELL

They sit, leaning back, against the foot of my bed.
I sit across from them and explain
everything:
      —how I discovered the envelope in the attic
      —how I found the note from Gramps
      —how I unfolded each of the maps
      —how I read the letter from the engineer
      —how I asked Mr. Bellamy about shifting rivers
      —how I'd been racking my tired brain for answers

I tell them about the key and about
the note Gramps wrote on the back of the envelope,
the one about the drawer, file, and document
over in Brigantine.
I tell them I've been wanting to go
to check it out
but have no way of doing so
without giving away Gramps' secret.

I tell them all of it. . . . Then I ask:
"So . . . what do you think?"

Malcolm nods slowly, continuously, like he's
one of those little dogs in the
back window of someone's Chevy.
He stays quiet.

Carolann stuffs a bunch of potato chips
into her mouth.
She chews, swallows, takes a swig
of her soda, swipes the back of her wrist
across her lips.

"Far out!" she says.

ASSUMPTION

I thought for sure
    that three brains
would be better
    than one.

I had assumed that
    as soon as I told
Carolann and Malcolm
    about Gramps' notes

and his maps,
    I'd immediately
feel relieved,
    that we'd immediately,

all three, together,
    see something obvious
that I, by myself,
    had missed.

I
    was
so
    wrong.

QUAKER OATHS

Before they leave
to go back home,
I make them both
swear on my
father's Bible
that they will
not tell a soul
about Gramps'
project, that they
will not say one
single word to
their parents
or their friends
or their brothers
or any future
boyfriends or
girlfriends they
might someday
have. I am not
worried about
Malcolm, who is
shy and quiet
by nature.
I am worried more
about Carolann
but not because
she would ever

mean to say
anything about
our secret
but it's just that
she's always
flitting here
and there
and it's in her
nature to share—
and so I make her,
even though her
parents raised her
as a Quaker
(and they don't
believe in taking
oaths), I make her
swear *twice*
on the Bible
just to be sure.

DIXON

Malcolm and I go shopping for
a couple of 45s at Bassline,
the record store
where Hairy Harry works part-time.
We buy "I Was Made to Love Her" by Stevie Wonder
and "Respect" by Aretha Franklin.

Then we walk next door to the five-and-dime
and buy ourselves two orange Creamsicles
and a copy of today's local news,
which we take the comics out of and use
to wrap up the records
for his brother's nineteenth birthday.

Dixon Dupree is the kind of brother
every kid should have:
he plays guitar, works at the lumberyard,
and last year as a senior at Willowbank High
he had fifteen home runs, thirty-five RBIs,
and was the team's MVP for the second time.

Plus Dixon's *nice* . . . a kind of anti-Denise.
Whenever I see him in town
or walking past our house after work,
Dixon always asks
how I am,
what I'm doing,

how's it going with my summer . . . stuff like that,
questions that most older kids
don't ask me.

Anyway, a few hours later,
when I arrive at the Duprees'
at half past seven
to watch the Phillies play the Mets on CBS,
Dixon is sitting on the top step of the porch,
reading a letter.

He does not
look up when I walk by.
He does not
say "Hey there, Lyza . . . ," like he always does.
He does not
ask how I am or if everything is cool with my summer.
Instead,
he keeps staring, staring, staring at the letter.

When Malcolm opens the door,
I can see over his shoulder into the kitchen,
where Mrs. Dupree is crying into her apron
with Mr. Dupree trying to comfort her,
and before I can turn and leave them
to whatever bad news it is,
Malcolm grips my wrist and pulls me
behind him upstairs to the den, directly
opposite his room.

When he turns around, I can clearly see
that he looks close to crying, too.
Now I am feeling really weird, 'cause I have not
seen Malcolm cry since kindergarten,
when the older white kids
teased and bullied him
through the playground fence.

"Dixon's got drafted," he says, sitting
down on the top of the desk, still looking like
he might explode into sadness any minute.

I don't know what to do.
I don't know what to say.

So I look instead
across the hall, over his bed,
at the poster of the late Dr. Martin Luther King, Jr.,
who's exactly the kind of person, every morning,
a kid should wake up to.

GRAY, WHITE, AND BLUE

I've had it starred on my calendar since December.
Every year at the high school, the town
puts on a big July Fourth fireworks show.
Everyone goes.

And because it's one of the few family
traditions we've kept since Mom
left, even Princess Denise
doesn't complain.

We get there an hour early, about eight,
and are greeted at the gate by a
small group of anti-war
demonstrators

waving signs that say: War Makes Men Dead!
and Get Them Out—NOW! I know Dad
is not for the war, but he is *for*
keeping his

full-time job at Glassboro State; he tries to
appear neutral in public so he doesn't
get into trouble with the college
administration.

Denise and Harry hang out with the protestors,
which makes me think for the first time

about Harry: he's twenty and not
a college guy,

so why, I wonder, hasn't he got drafted yet? We get
settled on our blanket in the middle of
the football field and buy
some sparklers

from the concession stand. Harry and Denise
come back and spread their tie-dyed sheet
next to us. Harry knows that Dad
lives in his own world

and that Denise doesn't care a lick if Harry's nice
to me or not. So I'm surprised when he
offers me some popcorn and a swig
of his Coke,

then asks what I've been up to since school's been done.
I dodge the question: "How come you're not
fighting in Vietnam?" I ask. Denise
hears and starts

to curse at me, but Harry holds up his hand. "I don't mind, Dee,"
he says to her, and then to me: "I'm color-blind, Lyza.
Turns out that those of us who can't tell
red from green

don't have to kill other young men who can—or at least,
not yet." I ask him if he heard about Dixon.

"Yeah, I did—he doesn't like this
war any more

than me, but he doesn't want to run off to Canada,
either, to get out of being drafted." Harry
shakes his head. "The whole
thing stinks. . . ."

Carolann's family arrives. They set their chairs
and blankets next to us, and as we're
twirling sparklers and watching
the first rockets

and pinwheels go off, I wonder: What must they look like
through Harry's color-blind eyes? And what would
he see inside my kaleidoscope?
Then I think maybe . . .

if I say a special prayer tonight, God might make
Dixon color-blind just long enough
to keep him home
from Vietnam.

Rockets flare; I see faces of neighbors that Mom
knows, too. I imagine her in some new park
watching fireworks like she used to
watch them here with us.

July Fourth was one of her favorite holidays. "Hooray
for parades, fireworks, and nothing but

hot dogs to cook," she'd say.
Now, when I

think of her twirling a patriotic pinwheel in some other
field in some other town (maybe even with
some other *family*), I wonder if she's
remembering me, too.

ROAD TRIP

"I got us a ride . . . over to Brigantine!"

This is Malcolm's out-of-breath announcement
as I open the front door
to let out the smoke from the meat loaf
that Denise is trying to bake.

"What's on fire?" he asks, still gasping.

"Nothing—that's just Denise trying to make
us dinner. . . ."

We sit on the front-porch step.
"What do you mean," I ask,
"about the ride to Brigantine?"

"It's with Dixon. He's got to go over near there
for his physical with the Army doc. He says we
can come, too. Tomorrow, ten o'clock."
We run across the street to tell Carolann,
whom we find in the backyard
being chased by the twins and their fully loaded
squirt guns.

"Tomorrow? Does it have to be *tomorrow?*" she asks us,
jogging by. "I can't. I promised my mother
I'd watch my brothers
while she's in Millville with my aunt."

Malcolm and I each grab a twin.
While they squirm and squeal, the three of us
argue a little over whether we should go anyway,
or wait. But even Carolann understands
there may not be another ride to Brigantine for a very long time.
"Plus Dixon doesn't care *why* we want to go,"
Malcolm reasons. "But if we ask someone's father
or mother to take us, they'll want to know."

Carolann gives in. "OK, go ahead without me.
But swear you'll tell me everything
as soon as you get back. . . ."

We swear on two Nancy Drew mysteries,
because that's what she has handy
and because, really,
Carolann takes them just as seriously.

AN OUNCE OF PREVENTION

I call Information to get the location
of the Historical Society in Brigantine.
The lady on the other end of the line
sounds a lot like my mother (but she isn't),
so I keep asking her to repeat what she
says just so I can listen to her nice voice.
"Right by the lighthouse, honey . . . you know,
that's where the tourists go the whole summer
season, so all you need to do when you get
here is look for that blasted beacon. . . ."
I thank her and hang up. Tomorrow, that
brass key is definitely coming with me. I'll bet
it will fit some door or drawer or cabinet
with some new clue in it. Now I have to
decide if I should take the maps with us
tomorrow or leave them home. Denise has
a habit of snooping through my room when
I'm gone; that's a good reason to bring them.
But we can't figure out this thing if they get
stolen, lost, or torn; that seems like a good reason
to leave them. I can't decide. I flip a coin:
heads, I bring them along; *tails*, I don't.
(It's tails.) I stuff them in my bottom drawer,
beneath my underwear, but then I'm not
so sure Denise won't go snooping there.
Hmmm. I decide to slide them behind

the schoolbooks on my shelf. I also write a
KEEP OUT sign, which I'll tape to my
door frame tomorrow, right before I go.
I know a sign won't begin to stop Denise—
but it might make her leave a little faster.

Part 4

It's gonna be a long, hard drag, but we'll make it.

—Janis Joplin, American singer

BODY LANGUAGE

I bounce
   down
      the steps

a little too	eagerly	when I see	the Duprees'
light blue	Chevy	pull up	Malcolm holds
the car door	open	for me	I slide into
the backseat	suddenly	remembering	that today
won't be	such a	good one	for Dixon.

RESEARCH

We arrive at 9:45,
read the little handwritten sign in the window:
    OPEN MONDAY THRU SATURDAY, 10 TO 6.
    SPECIAL SEA HORSE EXHIBIT JUNE 15–SEPT. 15.
We tell Dixon to go
so he doesn't miss his physical.

After he leaves, we feed the resident seagulls
a sleeve of saltines. We walk around the block,
come back at ten. An old man
with a long gray beard and skin as tan
as a coconut lets us in.

"You kids here for the sea horses?" he asks.

As usual when we meet someone new, someone who's
white, Malcolm hangs back, waiting to see
how the stranger will react.
The old man, whose suntan makes him
almost as dark as Malcolm, seems completely at ease.
His round cheeks and eyebrows thick as dune grass
remind me of Santa Claus. On one strap
of his overalls, there's a tag:
CHARLIE TUCKER, CURATOR.

He's fine, my look tells Malcolm, who moves
cautiously
away from the door.

"No, sir," I answer Mr. Tucker. "We're here to do
research." I hand him the slip of paper
on which I copied
the drawer, file, and document numbers
from the back of Gramps' envelope.
"Can you help us find this?"

Mr. Tucker's dune-grass eyebrows rise up together.
He strokes his beard with his left hand,
holds the paper under the nearest light
with his right. "Well . . . hmmm . . . this one's
upstairs . . . one of our oldest collections . . .
doesn't get looked at much . . . I've only had
one man
ask for it these past several years. . . ."

He looks up again at our faces. He's deciding.
Malcolm's foot is jittering. My stomach's fluttering.
Why didn't I think about this? What if
he doesn't let us see whatever it is
those numbers stand for?

"My father teaches at Glassboro State!" I blurt out,
hoping this might help.
Mr. Tucker seems interested. "He teach history?"

Now I have to lie.
But I decide this time it might be worth it.
I cross my fingers behind my back.

"Yep," I tell him. "He's home sick in bed,
so he sent us instead."

Now Malcolm's eyebrows, which are thin and straight
as toothbrush bristles,
rise up together. Mr. Tucker, however,
is convinced. "Come along, then," he says,
unlocking the dead-bolted door,
leading us up the staircase to the second floor.

LET THE RECORD SHOW

The second floor is dark. It has a row
of padlocked cabinets and two long tables
with reading lamps propped on top.

Mr. Tucker unlocks one of the cabinets,
takes out a brown leather-bound notebook,
hands us each a ballpoint pen. "You gotta sign

to look at the documents," he tells us as he
switches on our light. "These are the property
of the Historical Society—rules say I have to

keep track of who reads them and when."
Now both of Malcolm's feet are jittery, and my
stomach has moved up into my throat. We

exchange worried looks. *What are you
getting me into?* is what his look says. Mine says:
Was my gramps doing something crazy . . .

*or, even worse, something illegal? Is that
the real reason he wanted me to keep it secret?*
We both sign the book, give it back to Mr. Tucker.

Ready or not, we are about to find out.

FOR THE RECORD

Mr. Tucker opens another locked cabinet.
I finger the key in my own pocket,
wondering if it might fit any of the other
locked drawers up here. Meanwhile, Mr. Tucker
brings a thick black binder over
to the table, opens it to a yellow divider
that's marked in red pen: *Ships' Logs, 1680–1700*.

He flips through the plastic page covers,
stops at a certain spot, and slides the whole binder
in front of Malcolm and me.
"I'll be right there," he says, pointing to a chair
on the other side of the room. "Rules also say
I got to stay
whenever these files are open. And remember,
use a pencil for any notes you take—
no pens allowed."

We watch him walk over to the rocker,
pick up the newspaper on the cushion,
and make himself comfortable behind it.

"I thought your dad only taught math," Malcolm whispers.

"He does," I say. "But I didn't think Pythagoras
would get us too far with Mr. Tucker.

"Besides," I start to say, "this might be our only—"

"Sweet Jesus!" Malcolm whispers, tugging
on my T-shirt sleeve and pointing
to the date at the top
and the name at the bottom
of the ship's-log entry
on the plastic-covered page:

> June 3, 1699
> Captain William Kidd

ROUTE 9 NORTH

The ride back to
Willowbank takes

a lot longer. No one
talks. No one seems

to breathe. Dixon
passed his physical;

he reports for duty
next week. Malcolm

rocks his knees back
and forth, and my

stomach growls so
loud, Dixon turns

the radio up just
to drown it out.

I reach into my
pocket, feel around

for the piece of
notebook paper

on which I copied,
word for word,

exactly what
Captain Kidd, who

might be the most
famous pirate ever,

said in his ship's log
on June 3rd,

more than two hundred
fifty years ago.

When we stop
along Route Nine

for gas and snacks,
I read the headline

on the papers stacked
beside the station:

Casualties Increase
as Johnson Moves

to Boost American
Troops. Before Dixon

and Malcolm come
back outside, I slide

the papers behind
the air pump

on which someone
has drawn a green

peace sign and
written underneath:

HONK IF YOU
LOVE JANIS.

CAPTAIN MALCOLM KIDD

That night, we meet again in my room.
Denise is at the diner,
Dad's describing right triangles
to young men who have suddenly discovered
that going to college is one way to stay
out of Vietnam.

After I tell Carolann the details
of our trip to Brigantine, Malcolm reads out loud
every word
I copied from the pirate captain's log:

June 3, 1699:

*We are being pursued by a hostile vessel, most
probably of the Royal Navy. It appears that my
former identity as a loyal servant of Her Majesty
has been replaced by that of "Outlaw." So be it. The
St. Antonio can outrun and outmaneuver almost
any ship. But there is the problem, should bad luck
or poor weather befall us and prevent our escape, of
the chest. This I will put to the crew, who must
decide quickly if we are to anchor and go ashore
unnoticed.*

Captain William Kidd

June 4, 1699:

*We have sailed into the Great Bay, located about
fifty miles up the coast from the southernmost tip of
the New Jersey Colony. Our ship is hid well, though
not blocked from the open sea, should we need to
make our escape. The crew, after much argument,
has voted: First Mate Timothy Jones and I will
together take a small boat and the chest and row
several miles up the river that empties into this bay.
At a point mutually agreed upon, we shall land the
boat, bury the chest, mark its placement on paper,*

and return to the *St. Antonio*. After we lose our
pursuers, we shall come back with a few more
members of our crew and recover the treasure.

Captain William Kidd

June 6, 1699:

These past two days have tested me and my men in
ways I could not have imagined. At first, our
decision to hide the spoils of our latest raid, so as
not to let them fall into enemy hands should we be
overtaken, seemed prudent. At sunrise, Mate Jones
and I rowed upriver for several miles in search of a
suitable place to bury the booty. Then, just beyond
a slight leftward bend in the river, our rowboat
struck, with much force, a submerged tree, which
immediately ripped a large hole in her hull. Mate
Jones and I tried to keep the chest afloat as we
swam for the riverbank, but of course it was no use.
The river was swollen from recent rains, and we
were forced to swim for our lives while the chest
sank. Once we were safely ashore, however, Jones
began accusing me of planning this accident. We
argued; he drew his knife, intending to kill me, so as
to make himself captain as well as the only living
soul to know the location of the treasure. I was able
to stop him only by stabbing him in the heart with
his own weapon. He died straightaway. I dragged
Jones's corpse into the woods, covered it with leaves,
and returned to the river, so I could try to mark in

my memory where the chest went down. Then I walked back to the ship.

Upon hearing my story, the men were understandably skeptical. Having already endured one mutiny, I was in no hurry to encourage another. Thus I pledged to them that as soon as we are no longer being followed, we will come back to the river and recover the chest, and the crew will divide among themselves all of its contents. And I, in return for taking the life of Mate Jones, will claim none.

We make haste now for the open sea, as the Royal Navy has spotted us.

Captain William Kidd

REQUEST

It's weird to hear
a notorious pirate's words
coming out of Malcolm's mouth.
I have goose bumps on my arms, even more
than when I read those pages
silently
in Brigantine. Even more than when I copied them

down in pencil on notebook paper
(I write fast, but it still took me almost an hour)
as Mr. Tucker snored in his rocker
and Malcolm tiptoed from cabinet to cabinet
with the brass key that Gramps left me,
to see if it fit
in any of the other locks (it didn't).

Carolann, who is almost never at a loss for words,
is at a loss for words.
Finally, she asks: "Can I see those
three maps?"

NEVER UNDERESTIMATE YOUR NEIGHBOR

I pull the maps from their hiding place
in my bookcase.

Carolann unfolds them on the floor, walks
around them twice, then slides

the onionskin one of the Mullica River
in 1699 over the top of the current map

of Willowbank. (Why didn't *I* think of
that? The whole time I was trying to figure

all this out by myself, I was comparing
old river to new river, but never the

old river to new *town*. Sometimes
I think Denise is right and I am truly

an idiot.) Malcolm and me, we move
closer to see what she sees: that the

course of the river way back in 1699,
the year in which Captain Kidd's chest—

according to his ship's log—
sank somewhere in the middle, fits

exactly over the three places, A, B, C,
that Gramps marked down in town.

"Lyza, your gramps wasn't looking for
a house, he was looking for a treasure

that the most famous pirate ever
had lost and maybe never came back for."

Malcolm and me, we think on this
a minute. "How do we know for sure?"

I say. "Maybe he *did* come back for it
and there's nothing there. . . ." Malcolm

holds up the brass key. "My guess is this
is *not* from the seventeenth century. But if

it doesn't fit anything over in Brigantine,
then what's it for?" We hear someone

coming up the stairs. *Denise.*
Shoot! She's supposed to be at work.

The other two scramble to hide the maps
while I grab the blanket from my bed,

spread it across my door frame to block
my sister's prying eyes.

FEELING HER WHEATIES

Denise and I almost never eat together.
    This morning, however,
we end up in the kitchen at the same time.

Normally, I would just wait until later,
    until she and her *Female Power,*
Flower Power T-shirt are out of my way. But today,

as soon as it opens, Carolann and I are meeting
    Malcolm at the library, where we
hope to find out more about the fate of our

recently adopted pirate captain. Denise sits
    across the table, eating her Wheaties
and reading her women's-lib newsletter. I chomp

on a banana while my bread smokes in our
    one-sided toaster. Then Denise stops
reading and things get weird. Not only does she

seem pleased at my presence, she expresses her
    concern for my health and social habits:
"Lyza, you look tired, you look worried . . .

and I notice you're spending a lot of time
    in your room. . . ." Who is
this strange person across the breakfast table?

An analogy: Denise is to concern and empathy
    as Dad is to discipline.
As soon as she leaves, I drag some peppermint

Crest across my teeth, throw on my blue jeans,
    and run across the street
to get Carolann. As we walk the three blocks

to the Willowbank Public Library, I try to ignore
    a bad feeling that Denise—
somehow, some way—knows more than she should.

KIDD'S TALE

I think Mrs. Leinberger feels sorry for me because of Mom leaving
    and everything. She's always especially patient, even when
    I ask a lot of stupid questions or pull half the books off the
    shelf and don't even take them out. So naturally, my two
        best friends elect *me* to lead our little pirate inquiry
            at the library. Fine. Mrs. Leinberger is,

    of course, surprised to see three eager teenagers at her desk the
        second the doors open. "We'd like to know where to go to

find out more about pirates," I tell her. She leads us over to the
nonfiction section, to the 900s, trails her index finger
along the spines of one shelf of books. "Any of
these may help. Are you looking up any

particular pirate?" she asks. We talked about this last night, and we
decided that in case she starts asking about why we are all of a
sudden so interested in pirates, we would need to be careful.
I try to disguise our real goal. Here goes: "I think Black-
beard, Captain Tew, and maybe Captain Kidd, too."
Mrs. Leinberger leaves for a minute. We start
pulling some pirate books off the shelves.

When she comes back, she hands me a slim book with a tattered
blue cover, apologizing for not having biographies on all three of
the pirates I named. I look at the title: *The Life of William Kidd,
Reluctant Pirate*, written by H. A. McCue and published in
London in 1952. "Thanks, Mrs. L," I say. "I guess this
will just have to do."

SUMMER SCHOOL

We lie side by side in my backyard.
Our eyes and our minds are tired.
We stayed the whole day at the library

reading about pirates, and in particular
about Captain Kidd. So far, this is
what we know: William Kidd was

born in Scotland in 1654. His father,
who was a sailor, died when he was five.
Kidd grew up poor. As a teenager,

he ran off to try his own luck at sea.
He worked on many different ships, doing many
different jobs, sailing all over the world.

When Kidd became captain of an English ship,
he won an important battle against the French;
this made him sort of a war hero.

In 1691, he married Sarah Oort, and they had
two daughters: Elizabeth and Sarah. The Kidd family
lived in a nice house—on Wall Street!—in New York

(that was Carolann's favorite part). The captain
had an honest and excellent reputation
with just about everyone. Until 1695,

he lived a quiet, settled life. But then . . .
the governor of New York and some other
businessmen formed a plan: they sent Kidd

on a ship to the Indian Ocean with a piece of paper
that said he was allowed to *hunt for and attack*
pirate ships, and in return, they would share

the loot with him (the book explained that this
was called *privateering*). Kidd did this—
sort of. At some point in the long sea journey,

when Kidd refused to attack another ship
carrying valuable cargo, his crew—many
of whom were former pirates—staged a mutiny.

They tried to kill Captain Kidd. Luckily,
he was able to defend himself, but had no choice,
if he wanted to *live*, than to convert to piracy

(that was Malcolm's favorite part; since his
father's an evangelistic minister, he's seen
more than his share of conversions). This happened

again and again over the next several years:
the captain would *try* to follow the principles
of privateering and to attack only *certain*

kinds of ships. But his crew, who wanted
more and bigger loot, would overrule him
and attack almost any ship they could.

According to the books we read, Kidd
was really an honest man, a respectable
sea captain, and a truly reluctant pirate.

When Kidd tried in 1699 to come home
to his family in New York, he left his big
ship, the *Quedagh Merchant*, in the Caribbean,

took a smaller, faster vessel, and sailed cautiously
up the east coast of the American colonies, including
Virginia, Maryland, Delaware, and New Jersey.

Kidd knew his outlaw reputation had spread.
So, according to some of his crew, he stopped
now and then to bury some of his treasure

in case he needed some reason to persuade
the governor not to arrest him. (This was when
he would have made his trip up the Mullica.)

When he reached New York, he collected his
family and sailed on to Boston, where the very
men who'd backed his mission turned against him

(this was my favorite part; desertion seems to be
my specialty), handing him over to the British
courts. Poor Captain Kidd spent more than a year

in a filthy English prison before he was granted
a trial. In May of 1701, he was convicted of piracy
and hanged. His body was displayed in a cage

over the Thames River for two whole years
as a warning to any captain or sailor who
might consider piracy. It appears that Kidd

never came back to America,
which means . . . he never collected
any of his buried treasure.

Part 5

How many children must we kill
Before we make the waves stand still?
                                    —from "Saigon Bride"
                            by Nina Dusheck and Joan Baez

ONCE AGAIN

I don't want to go.
Neither does Denise.
It's still too soon. Too sad.
We each make excuses to Dad—

Denise: "It's Harry's birthday. We have tickets
to a show, and he'll be so bummed if we can't go!"

Me: "I promised Malcolm and Carolann I'd spend
the day with them, doing—you know—stuff."

Dad looks at us both, square, runs his hand
through his rapidly graying hair. "Denise," he says,
"you can stay to celebrate with Harry.
Lyza, you need to go, but tell your friends
they're welcome to join us in Tuckahoe
as long as they don't mind helping out at the auction."

Dad leaves to teach a class. Denise does
a victory dance down the hall. I call Malcolm

and Carolann to tell them they've won
a deluxe one-day vacation
in Tuckahoe, round-trip transportation
included.

JULY 13, 1968

"Tables, rugs, lamps, bookcases, garden tools,
blankets, chairs—everything goes to the highest bidder!"

the auctioneer declares from his perch on the back porch.
Malcolm and Carolann help us keep everything coming

to the auction block, where it's sold at bargain prices
to total strangers. It's hard to watch. Even though I know

we have no use for any of it, it's still hard to watch. At lunch,
I don't say much. I sit in Gramps' favorite chair on the lawn,

flip through some of his old magazines and play with my
kaleidoscope. My friends understand. Carolann squeezes

my hand and Malcolm feeds me Cracker Jacks he's brought
from home. We're almost through by half past two. Dad brings

the last things from the basement, including a broken rocker
and a blue-painted steel locker with a padlock on the front.

As Dad wheels them past in a wooden wagon, Malcolm starts
waving his arms like a willow in a storm. "You see the lock?

It says *The Benson Company*—that's what it says across
the top of the brass key you showed me, the one your

grandfather taped to the back of that envelope!" Something
lurches in my throat. "How much money you got?" I ask.

Malcolm fishes in both his pants pockets for loose change.
He turns up eighty-five cents. We ask Carolann. "I brought

my June allowance—four dollars," she says. I search every
pocket of my overalls: two dollars, ten cents. The bid is up

to five bucks. We bid six. Someone says *six fifty*. We say
six ninety-five—all we have. The next minute is three

hours long. Finally, the gavel bangs and the auctioneer
points to us: "One steel blue locker . . . contents unknown . . .

SOLD! . . . to the young buyers in the front row!" We run up
and wheel the thing away before he changes his mind.

NOT EXACTLY A JOYRIDE

We tell Dad we need the locker
               for a summer project (which is true).
He just shakes his head and says:
               "My father, the family pack rat . . . I guess
it's pretty typical for him to keep
               something huge and useless like this. Where
in the world will you guys *put* it?"
               I've seen hundreds of pouty I-might-cry-at-
any-minute-Daddy looks on Denise's face.
               I'm desperate: I try my own version now. He sighs.
"OK, OK. You win. But you'll have to sit
               in the way back and keep it from tearing up
the inside of the station wagon."
               No problem, we answer. *No sweat.*
Except . . . the locker is metal
               and it is heavy as a house and it has
a few sharp edges that keep digging
               into our legs every time we hit a bump
and when we turn a corner it
               shifts to the opposite side of the car
and whoever's side that is
               gets *squished* against the window.
By the time we reach Willowbank,
               we are so beat up, we leave the locker
in the car, run for the freezer,
               where we fill three plastic bags with

ice and sit on my front porch
                    healing our almost-seven-dollar wounds.

THE WONDERS OF MODERN TECHNOLOGY

It's another two days before
we can get together again
in a private place. This is
pretty important because
you can fold up three maps
pretty quick, but we don't know
what's in the locker with
the Benson Company padlock
on it, and just in case it is
something we don't want
anyone else to see, we wait
to meet at night in Carolann's
basement, where her father
helps us carry the heavy-
as-a-house locker down
the stairs. "A project, huh?"
he asks us, to which
Carolann responds with all
her charm: "Daddy, will you

PLEEEEase keep the twins
away from this—I need my
own space for things now that
I'm older," and to my surprise,
he agrees. We wait until he's
upstairs again watching the
evening news. I have the key
and we draw straws to see
who gets to try the lock first.
Malcolm draws the shortest straw
but he puts the key in my hand.
"I think you should open it, Lyza.
It's your granddad," he says.
Carolann nods. "Go ahead."
I slip the key carefully into
the lock. I try turning it left
but the lock is stiff. I turn it
right and pull down so that
the arm clicks open. I notice
my hand is shaking slightly
and my throat feels dry but I
remove the lock from the hole
in the metal door. I lift the latch
and pull. Inside is something
that looks like a shorter version
of the contraption that the
lifeguards use to clean the pool
at the Willowbank YWCA.
We all stand there looking.

"What *is* it?" Carolann finally asks.
Malcolm reaches in and pulls it
out. It has a long handle and
a battery pack and some kind
of round disk on the bottom,
about the size of an LP record.
"Malcolm, what *is* it?" I echo.
Malcolm inspects the battery
pack. He runs his hand down the
shaft to the round disk. Finally,
he answers. "I've seen these
before, at the hardware store . . .
people buy these to take
with them to the beach.
See this disk? They sweep it
back and forth over the sand—
try to find dropped coins
and jewelry and stuff. I'm
pretty sure it's some sort
of metal detector." Malcolm
grins. "Seems your gramps
was getting ready to find
that treasure chest before
he died. Now it's up to
you." I correct him quick:
"Up to *us*," I say. The door
at the top of the stairs opens
and Mrs. Mott calls down:
"Lyza, honey, your father's

on the phone. He wants you
to come home now." My *father*?
On the phone? For *me*? I give
Malcolm the key. "Lock up
when you're done," I tell him.
Then to Carolann: "You two
talk, then call me later and
we'll decide what to do next."
I take the stairs two at a time.
Dad never cares where I am.
He never calls when I'm with
Carolann's family. So this
can only mean one thing:
someone else is dead.

THE REAL MEANING OF IRONY

"Lyza . . . can you come in here a minute, please?"
That's Dad, calling me
into the living room as soon
as the front door shuts.

I go in and sit down
on the beat-up blue couch. Denise is there, too,

flipping through her paperback copy
of *Profiles in Feminism*, stretched out in the shaggy
orange chair that used to be Mom's.
Sometimes when I sit there watching *The Ed Sullivan Show*
or *Laugh-in* or *Carol Burnett*,
I think I can still smell the vanilla scent
Mom always wore to work.

Dad looks tired. I wonder why he's not
teaching tonight. I wonder
who has died this time. His fingers
are laced together on his lap.
He opens and closes them quickly
as if he's demonstrating butterfly wings
to a five-year-old.
(Not a good sign—much more serious than when
he runs his hand through his hair
or nervously clicks his tongue.)

"What's up?" I ask, trying to sound casual, trying
not to think about having to wear
that black dress again.

Dad leans forward. He rests his wrists
on his knees, his tangled fingers still spastically
opening and closing.
He glances at Denise, who nods
for him to continue. (Why is *she* here?
And what does she know that I don't?)

"Lyza . . . I'll get right to the point.
I realize I'm not here to oversee your activities
most of the time . . . maybe that's not right.
Maybe you should have some
adult supervision
more often."

I shrug. I ask the obvious question:
"Why? I do fine.
I finish my chores. I stay out of trouble.
If I really need anything, I can always
go over to the Motts' or the Duprees'."

"Lyza . . ." Dad shifts uneasily in his seat.
"Denise tells me you've been
spending a lot of time in your room. She says you seem
edgy,
     tired,
          nervous,
and sometimes you're having trouble
sleeping at night."

I shrug again. Maybe no one's died this time.
"Only when I forget and drink
too much Coca-Cola after dinner," I tell him.

"And you're hiding things," he adds,
"and making excuses to go off with your friends
in private."

I glare at Denise. If she knows about the maps,
and if she told Dad . . .

"Lyza . . ." Dad frowns like he's in pain.
Whatever he needs to say is stuck
halfway up his throat. Finally, he delivers:
"Lyza, Denise thinks you're doing drugs."

My ears hear, but my mind tries
to find another, saner meaning
for what my father is saying.

"Drugs?" I laugh. I point across at Denise.
"*She* . . . is accusing *me* . . . of doing drugs?"

I laugh harder now. This must be one of those
catch-you-in-the-act TV stunts.
I look around for Allen Funt
and his candid camera. This is just
unbelievable: not only is no one else dead,
not only does my wing-nut sister
not suspect anything
about Gramps' maps, but Princess Bradley
of the midnight roof rendezvous,
of the gauze shirts and miniskirts,
of the weed-toting, ponytailed, record store–employed boyfriend
thinks *I'm* doing drugs!

I can't stop. I hold my sides. I bend over
double. I gasp for breath.
"I'm sorrr—rry, Daddy," I manage to say through tears
of hysteria. "It's *j-jusst too f-f-funny.*"

NEVER UNDERESTIMATE YOUR STUPID SISTER

Somewhere in the Great Parenting Book
there must be a page that explains
how hysteria equals guilt.
Whoever wrote it should be shot.

Unfortunately for me, it must be the only page
my dad has read, because since
our little family meeting last night, he is convinced
I'm experimenting with drugs,
and no amount of my explaining and pleading
can convince him otherwise.

It would have been so easy to tell him
what I've *really* been doing—about Gramps' note,
the key, the maps, the locker, and the metal detector—

all of that.
I did, for a minute, consider it.

But then, in the end, it was one memory
that held me back: Gramps' photos of his
solo trip
from Florida to Maine, the way he'd said:
"I'd never felt more alive" and the way Dad, later on
in the car, had said: "Darn fool!"

In that moment I had to decide
to stay safe in the harbor, like my father,
or to push out to sea, like Gramps.

The decision was easier than I thought:
I kept my mouth shut.

Since then, Dad has concluded that I need more
"structured activities," more "adult supervision,"
more "accountability."
Why, of all times, did Dad have to pick
this summer to watch over me?

Denise, meanwhile, is sporting an annoying smirk.
I think she made all this up
just to torment me, just to exercise
her older-sister power over me
while she still can.

I hate Denise. I hate Janis Joplin. I hope she trips
on one of her ugly feather boas
and stays in a coma
for the next forty years. (I don't mean that, really.
OK, yes I do. Well, maybe not Janis.
Maybe Denise. Yes. *Denise*. If *she* trips
and ends up in a coma, I am never
coming to visit her.)

THE NEXT MORNING

I break the bad news about my father's plan
to Malcolm and Carolann:

"Tomorrow at nine o'clock sharp,
I report to Mr. Archer at the diner

to start my dishwashing job. I'll work
three days a week, nine to four-thirty,

and every Saturday night. When I'm not
at my job, Dad's made a list of chores

for me to do at home; he plans
to call the house and check on me

during his teaching breaks." Malcolm
can't believe it. Neither can Carolann.

"Want me to talk to your dad? He's always
liked me," she suggests. I shake my head.

"Thanks, but I don't think he'd listen. Dad's
equation is 'chores plus job equals no free

time for Lyza, equals no worries' for him.
I guess we'll have to figure a way around this."

I look at Malcolm, the quiet, thoughtful one.
"Any bright ideas?"

DISHPAN HANDS

I have been the main dishwasher
    at our house ever since Mom left.
So, my job training at the diner
    takes about six and a half minutes. Tops.

"Dishes first, cups next, glasses and silver-
     ware last," Mr. Archer instructs. I learn fast.

As I soap and rinse, I think about Malcolm's
     face when I told him I'd be
working here. He'd tried a few times
     to apply for a position in the kitchen—
cooking, washing, stocking—but Mr. Archer
     doesn't hire blacks. Period.

By my lunch break at quarter past two,
     I am keeping pace with the other washers,
Robert and Mary Sue. I grab a grilled ham
     sandwich and slip out the back to where
Malcolm and Carolann are already waiting
     in the alley. "Well . . . did it work?" I ask

through a mouthful of rye bread and mustard.
     Carolann hands me a jar full of pennies with
dirt smeared all down the side. "We buried this in
     a sandy spot in my yard and covered it real
good. The metal detector picked it up every time!"
     Malcolm smiles. (It was his idea.) "But . . . ,"

Carolann continues, "*both* my neighbors saw us
     dragging something big under my father's
tarp. We had to wait till they were gone to uncover
     the detector and test it over the penny jar."
Malcolm speaks up: "It won't be easy to hide

this thing once we start taking it to the three
spots your Gramps marked on that map."

I finish my ham sandwich. Carolann starts
　　pacing. I hand her the potato chips that came with it
to try and keep her still. Malcolm's right. We can't
　　drag that thing all around town, dig holes in the park or
at the school, and expect no one to notice. The back door

opens and Mary Sue steps into the alley to light a
　　cigarette. "We'll have to work after dark," I say
as we move further upwind, away from her smoke.
　　"And we'll have to be quick so I can make it
back for my dad's calls." It's time to get back to work.
　　"Be on my porch at eight-thirty," I whisper.

"But let's leave the detector at home tonight.
　　We can try to find points A and B and see
if they even exist and what's around them.
　　Then we can pick another time to find C."
They both agree. We say good-bye and as I

watch them walk away, Carolann chattering about
　　God-knows-what, Malcolm patiently
listening, I wonder if I *would* do drugs if I didn't
　　have them around me every day.

POINT A

Denise is working the evening shift at the diner. My father
is teaching a statistics class from seven
till ten-fifteen.

He calls me at eight-thirty to check in. "Everything all right?
You keeping up with those chores?"
Yes, Dad. Yes.

I've alphabetized all of his office files; I've vacuumed the
living room and mopped the kitchen floor,
twice. If he

makes his chore list any longer, I may need a few Cokes
just to stay awake. At exactly
eight-thirty-five,

Malcolm and Carolann and I take the Willowbank town map
to the spot Gramps marked
"Point A,"

which we find smack in the middle of the playground
behind Willowbank Elementary,
directly under

the jungle gym. Besides a pair of slowly strutting crows,
no one is around. "At least it's
not paved over,"

Carolann points out, climbing up the ladder to get a better
view. I climb up the other side
and look down at

Malcolm, who is drawing a circle on the ground with his
left foot. "But if we have to dig
a hole here, there is

no way we can cover it up again without someone noticing,"
he says. "Or without some little kid
falling in," Carolann adds.

"OK," I say. "Point A is easy to get to, but too exposed."
I check my watch: five past nine. Dad said he'd
call again before ten.

The crows squawk and scatter as we climb down the
jungle-gym ladder. Malcolm folds up the map
and we hightail it to the park.

B IS FOR BAD LUCK

It's completely dark. The few people left in the park
are walking out. We wander in to wait
under one of the little picnic pavilions.

When everyone else is gone,
Carolann holds the map under a flashlight
and barks out orders:

"Lyza, walk off sixty feet from the north corner
of the stone wall! . . . Malcolm, you measure
forty-five feet from the row of willows along the river!
. . . OK, now where you meet is Point B!"

We each take a flashlight and a tape measure
and do exactly as she says. We meet in the center
of another roof-covered picnic pavilion,
which sits upon two feet
of solid concrete.

Carolann comes running with the map.
"Well . . . unless your grandfather left you another locker
with a jackhammer in it, I'd say we need to pray
that this spot is *not*
where Captain Kidd lost that chest."

"The way my luck's been lately," I say,
"this is probably *exactly* where it's buried."

But now I don't have time
to do anything about it.
It's nine-forty-two
and my father is going to be calling home
any minute.

BREAK

We do nothing about the maps
or the treasure chest for the next two days.

Carolann watches the twins again
so her mother can visit her aunt in Millville.

I do more around-the-house chores, watch TV,
avoid Denise, and wash dishes at the diner.

Malcolm waits outside the barber shop
while Dixon gets his beautiful Afro shaved off.

Then they go fishing together all afternoon,
and even after the sun goes down, in the muddy

and ever-shifting Mullica River.

SUFFRAGE ON THE HIGH SEAS

Carolann calls to tell me
that she's been reading up on pirates
while she baby-sits.
According to her books, there were actually
a few feisty female bandits
who sailed the seas
around the same time as Captain Kidd.
(I wonder if the women's-libbers know this. . . .)

And two of these robber ladies—
Mary Read and Anne Bonny—
sailed and smuggled, robbed and killed
right along with their men
(Anne lived with the notorious Jack Rackham,
also known as "Calico Jack" because of his
patchwork pants) across the Atlantic and Pacific,
the Indian and Caribbean.

According to Carolann, one male pirate wrote:
    None among our crew
    were more resolute, or ready to . . .
    undertake anything that was hazardous.
Which means, I guess, that Anne and Mary
were as courageous and brave in battle
as anyone.

Carolann says those women were also
brainy. When finally caught and sentenced to hang

for their many deeds of piracy,
both Anne and Mary "pleaded for their bellies"
and were released from the scaffold
when the judge discovered
that each of them carried inside
a little pirate child.

NOT MUCH

When someone you love
    leaves,

and there is
    nothing   nothing   nothing

you can do about it, not one thing
    you can say to

stop that person whom you love
    so much

from going away, and you know that today
    may just be

the very last time you will ever
    see them   hear them   hold them,

when that day comes, there is not much
    you can do,

not much you can say. This morning, Dixon left
    for boot camp.

Soon, the Army's told him, he'll be on a plane
    to Vietnam.

Malcolm did not come out of his house until
    after dark,

when I watched him run past our house
    full-out,

his arms and legs pumping like pistons
    down Gary Street

to the park, where he disappeared behind
    the two long rows

of moonlit willows that waved their
    thin arms

in the evening breeze like so many children
    saying good-bye.

Part 6

Help me get my feet back on the ground.
Won't you please, please help me. . . .

—from "Help!"

by John Lennon and Paul McCartney

JUST A DREAM

Tonight while Harry
and Denise are seeing
Janis Joplin (in person)
scream into her
microphone and my
father is preaching
Pythagorean theory
in a classroom
at Glassboro State,
we three plan to meet
behind Mr. Dupree's
A.M.E. Church on
Mulberry Street
to see if Point C
is out in the open
or under two feet
of solid concrete.
After work I take
my kaleidoscope
to the porch, aim it
at the headlights of

passing cars to create
a kind of psychedelic
light show. Even so,
for about half an hour,
I fall asleep in
the wicker rocker;
I dream that Denise
is buried neck-deep
in playground dirt
and that my mother
is hiding somewhere
under the Mullica River
and that Carolann,
Malcolm, and me get
drafted to Vietnam
but when we arrive,
all we find is a field
full of holes and one
old treasure chest filled
with human bones.

C IS FOR CHURCH

After only one week of putting his
New and Improved Parenting Plan into effect,
my father is already
so predictable,
I can plan my evening outings
to the minute.

He calls at eight-thirty . . . *precisely* at eight-thirty.
   Yes, Dad.
      Yes, I finished that, too.
         Yes, I'm in the living room, reading.
            Yes, I know Denise won't be home until late.
            Yes, I know you're working late, too.
          Yes, I'll lock up.
           Yes. Good night.
After that first night, he does not call twice.

Carolann arrives at eight-thirty-five,
Malcolm at eight-forty.
At precisely eight-forty-five, we carry
the metal detector, wrapped in a blanket,
down Gary Street two blocks,
turn right onto Walnut,
and make our way over to Mulberry,
to the side yard
of the A.M.E. Church.

We rest beside the back door to the sanctuary,
where every Sunday the A.M.E. gospel choir
praises the Savior
and where, every Sunday till now,
Dixon Dupree's deep bass voice
has led them in song.

I turn to Malcolm. "Is there anyone around?"
He shakes his head. "Dad's at home and
no one else comes here
on weeknights. We should be fine."
We unwrap
the metal detector and draw straws to see
who gets to use it, who gets to read the map,
and who gets to stand guard.

I go last and draw
the shortest,
which means I get to suit up. Malcolm helps me
strap on the battery pack,
clip on the headphones,
and activate the magnetic signal.
Carolann stands guard in the yard.
"OK," Malcolm says, pulling out the map
and a tape measure.
"I'll walk off thirty-nine feet from the
building's cornerstone and hold the tape.
From there, you head northwest, toward the woods,
another eighty-eight feet."

I do as Malcolm says. He holds the tape on
the pivot spot
while I head off into the pines
behind the church.

At about eighty feet, I begin to swing the detector
back and forth   in front of me,   just like we
   saw one of our   American   soldiers do
the other night   on TV   when he   was using
   one of these to   check a field for   f r a g m e n t a t i o n
mines before   he led his men   across.

NOT EXACTLY EASY LISTENING

I stop counting at eighty-seven. I'm standing

beside a fallen

maple tree about ten feet into the woods

and the signal

is so strong I think I might go deaf

if I can't

get these stupid headphones off!!

TWO SIDES TO EVERY COIN

Yesterday after dark,
while I was still washing dishes at the diner
to cover a shift for Mary Sue, who
had a bad ear infection

(or so she told Mr. Archer—
I think she drove down to the beach;
she's pretty darn tan for a full-time dishwasher),

Malcolm and Carolann went back to Point A,
under the jungle gym at the playground,
and took the metal detector with them.

Yesterday after dark,
Malcolm and Carolann made sure

no one else was around
(not even the crows this time) before they wore

the headphones, switched on the instrument,
and swept it back and forth over
the top of the spot where the map said
the treasure might be.

Yesterday after dark,
the metal detector picked up
something
under the jungle gym, but the signal wasn't as strong
as the one behind the church. So Carolann

used her shoes to scoop up sand
and there she found a quarter, two nickels, and four
shiny pennies (a grand total of thirty-nine cents),
probably dropped by unsuspecting mothers or upside-

down, knee-hanging kids. Then Malcolm
and Carolann swept the spot again, and this time:
no signal. So—unless the treasure is under
the cement floor of the picnic pavilion in the park

(and if it is, we may never know . . .),
there seems to be no reason why we shouldn't
start digging at Point C in the woods
behind the A.M.E. Church tomorrow evening.

If Mary Sue's ear is still "infected" then,
I'm going to tell Mr. Archer
he'll have to wash the dirty dishes
himself.

THE GOOD, THE BAD, THE UNTHINKABLE

The rain is coming down hard and fast,
like a Jimi Hendrix guitar riff.

Tonight we had planned to start digging,
but instead we are sitting

in Carolann's family's Volkswagen van,
watching the drops hit the windshield

and the rolled-up windows and hearing the
rat-a-tat-rat-a-tat on the metal roof

while we sit in the backseat and make
a list of things that are good and bad

about the location of Point C.
So far, this is what we've got:

GOOD: The detector says there is something metal buried in the
   woods.
BAD: It's not so far *into* the woods that it will be well hidden if
   we have to dig a really big hole.

GOOD: Both Malcolm's mom and Carolann's dad are
   gardeners—so getting shovels will not be a problem.
BAD: If the treasure is large (it sank pretty fast in the river,
   according to Captain Kidd's log), it will take *a lot* of digging;
   we can't go out there every night without our families
   getting suspicious. So . . . we'll have to take turns, spread out
   our visits. So . . . this *could* take us the rest of the summer.

GOOD: We don't have school, so losing a lot of sleep won't be a
   big problem.
BAD: Malcolm and Carolann's families will mostly be home at
   night. They'll need to sneak out or lie (probably both) to
   get over to the church unnoticed.

GOOD: When there are three of us, two can dig and one can
   stand watch.
BAD: Even with all of that digging, if the chest is buried under a
   lot of soil and sand, someone might notice us before we
   find it.

GOOD: The metal detector's signal was so strong, we are almost
   guaranteed to find *something*.
BAD: The instrument might be picking up the metal on the
   outside of the chest (we saw pictures of pirate chests in the

library books; they're mostly made of wood, with iron nails and locks). Inside, there might be nothing that's valuable anymore. Carolann has been reading about how things like salt, pepper, licorice, and cinnamon were worth a lot of money in pirate times. . . . We try not to think about going through all this for a bunch of condiments.

GOOD: If we find an actual treasure, we might be rich forever. And if we don't, at least we killed a few weeks of summer, spent some time together, and kept ourselves from thinking about ninth grade, nuclear bombs, and Vietnam.

(That's not so bad.)

AWOL

We arrive around nine.
Carolann went to bed early "with a headache,"
then she
climbed
down
the
tree
outside her room.

Malcolm told his mom he was staying
over at Jeremy Brown's house. He's brought
two shovels from his mom's garden shed, which we'll hide
somewhere near the church
when we're done digging.
Then, Malcolm figures, he'll sneak inside—
through the back window—
and find a good place to sleep.

My father called home at eight-thirty.
He probably won't call again. So—
I have about two hours
before Dad or Denise comes home.

We roll aside the fallen tree,
lift the flat rock that marks the spot
where the detector's signal was strongest.
While Carolann stands watch,
Malcolm and me tie our flashlights
in the V of a nearby tree
and start to dig.

CHAIN-GANG BLUES

Now I understand why pirates
in all the TV movies
usually bury their treasure
on flat, treeless beaches,

and why convicted criminals
are sentenced to hard labor
on chain gangs where they
dig ditches dawn till dusk.

The three of us have been
taking turns digging every
other night for a week,
and we have hit more rocks

and tree roots than we care
to count. Sometimes just two of us
can come, sometimes it's all three.
So far, though, no one has noticed

when we're gone or when we slip
back home late, late at night.
So far, no one has noticed the
three-foot-wide by two-foot-deep

hole behind the A.M.E. Church,
which we carefully cover with

the fallen tree, a big piece of plastic,
and several leafy branches.

My shoulders ache; I have
blisters on my fingers
and my palms, which
sting like crazy whenever

I plunge them into the hot
dishwater at the diner;
so to keep myself from
yelling out loud whenever

my hands hit the suds,
I have begun to sing
"Me and Bobby McGee"
while I'm working, and since

blues goddess Janis yells
at least as much as she sings,
no one in the kitchen is
the least bit suspicious.

A HEAVENLY GAME

We only get one chance
to dig this week.

Carolann's aunt from Millville
is here for a visit,

which means Carolann has to give up
her room and sleep on the couch,

where it would be hard *not* to notice
if she tried to sneak out at night.

Malcolm and me, we do our best to
switch off digging and standing watch,

but then, just our luck, the church
decides to have its summer picnic

in the side yard (the Duprees always
invite me), so all we can do that day

is stand about thirty yards
from our carefully covered hole

and nibble on corn dogs, coleslaw,
baked beans, and chocolate cake.

After we eat, all the kids play baseball,
with home plate being near the back door

and left field being right in front
of the trees that stand about ten feet

from our dig. Malcolm and me make sure
we get on different teams and we make

really sure that we each play left field
(which isn't easy, since everyone knows

Malcolm's a pretty good pitcher) and we
scramble, sprint, and dive for every

hit that comes anywhere near us.
Then I slip—a hit gets past me . . .

I run till I think my lungs will burst
while the ball rolls right into the woods by

our hole. I say a quick prayer under my
breath, and when I get there, the plastic

has stopped it from dropping in.
I grab it and run back toward

the game. I heave it as hard as I can
to the infield (so much for healing

my aching shoulders) while I make
a promise to God that if we *do* find

a treasure, I will come to church again
and I will even pray for Janis Joplin

—and maybe Denise.

VACANCY

Another week of digging.
More blisters.
Shoulders ache.

Still
a big,
empty   hole.

UNEXPECTED

I am walking past the cemetery gate
on my way to work at the Willowbank Diner
when I see Harry Keating pulling weeds
from around one headstone,
then moving on to do the same

to another. I stop to watch and then—
I don't know why—I decide to go in and say hi
to Harry and that's when I see that he's
taking care of Eddie's, Guy's, and Charley's graves.
Now I'm thinking maybe I have been

too quick to label Harry as lazy, to lump
him in with some of the other older
teens in town whose only occupation
is complaining. Harry looks up. "Hey, Lyza."
"Hey," I say. I help him pull dandelions

from around the stones, and we talk about
stuff happening in town, about a few of the new
music groups, about him filling in for Dixon
at the lumberyard. "The old guys tease me
about my ponytail," he says. "But I like the work."

The more we talk, the nicer Harry seems.
So I ask him, flat out, how he puts up
with Denise. He laughs, but even *he*

must see what a pain she can be sometimes.
"I know she seems unreasonable . . . but
Denise really does care about you, Lyza—
she just has trouble showing it."

I tell Harry that I think his color-blindness
is affecting his judgment with women.
I tell him that as long as he's going to
hang around with my sister, I wish he
would go ahead and marry her, get her

out of our house and my hair. Harry
laughs again, but then he gets serious.
"Maybe someday, I'll actually do that."
(Jeez—the thought of Hairy Harry
and Denise getting hitched is just *weird*.)
After this, we walk over to where

Gramps is buried. The headstone says:
LEWIS BRADLEY, 1888–1968.
It needs weeding, too. So Harry and me,
we both kneel down, start to pull out
the vines and thistles that have grown
on either side. This hurts my digging blisters,
which I'm doing my best to hide from Harry.
I try not to remember the funeral. I try
not to think about everyone I've lost . . . but
of course that's exactly where my mind goes.

Suddenly I can't see the weeds in front of me.
My eyes fill up and even though I think
I can hold my tears back, in about two seconds
I am sobbing into Harry's long brown hair,
which smells like sawdust and cigarettes, while he

holds me, letting me be sad for as long
as I need. I never thought I'd say this,
but if Harry marries Denise,
at least there will finally be someone
in the family I can lean on.

AIRMAIL

Malcolm shows me a letter from Dixon:

> Hey, Malcolm—
>   Well, we made it all the way across the world to
> South Vietnam. Now we wait to get our orders.
> Rumor has it they send blacks to where the fighting is
> worse. Every one of us is scared, but of course no
> one's saying so. Our base is right near the runway
> and you wouldn't believe the noise. Planes and
> choppers coming and going all the time. Lots of
> flag-covered caskets heading home.

My best friend here is a guy named William from Philadelphia. We call him Penn. He calls me Beach 'cause he thinks everyone from South Jersey must live right on the ocean. I don't mind, though. Having a nickname makes us seem more like a bunch of guys getting ready to play baseball.

So far, we run drills, play cards, clean our guns, and sleep when we can. I guess that'll all change in a few days, though. But don't worry . . . I'll be fine. I'll be home before the next Phillies season starts. But you got to watch them for me this year, OK? Take good care of Mom and Dad—and say hi to the neighbors.

Yours from the runway,

Dixon

MAD AT GOD

Malcolm came over today after lunch
to help me finish my chores.
Now here we are on the bench before
Miller's grocery store, sucking down
Fudgsicles, watching the traffic,
glancing through the *South Jersey News*.
Even though it's over one hundred degrees,

it feels like heaven to me: I'm off from
the diner, I have a whole two hours *free*.
"Look at this," Malcolm says, nudging me,
pointing the nearly empty stick of his Fudgsicle
at the picture on the front page. The photo
shows a pair of blood-covered Marines
being dragged by their buddies toward
a waiting chopper. Both guys look pretty
bad. "How can I believe in a God that puts
my brother in the middle of that?" he asks.
I don't answer. Not because I don't want to . . .
but because I don't know how. Since Mom left,
we haven't been back to Willowbank Episcopal,
where she and Dad were married and where
Denise and I were baptized. I hadn't
thought about God all that much until Gramps . . .
and until this summer, when it seems like—
given the total mess we humans have made—
even God could be forgiven for taking an
extended vacation. (That's what I'd do, too,
in His place.) But it's different for Malcolm,
being a minister's son and all. He still goes
to church each week, but he's been mad
at God ever since Dixon left for Vietnam.
And can you blame him? I study the photo
of those bloody (and young!) Marines,
who are sons and brothers, uncles and cousins
to people just like Malcolm and me. When
I can't stand it anymore, I flip quickly

to page three and read our horoscopes
silently. "What's it say?" Malcolm wants
to know. I lick the last of my Fudgsicle
from the stick and read our future (we're
both Scorpios) according to Zodiac Sally:
"You will be repaid for your sacrifice.
Be patient. See things through to the end."
I look up at Malcolm, whose toothbrush
eyebrows are raised in amazement.

ROOTS

We have hit a layer of shale
and some huge tree roots.

Before we dig any further, we bring
the metal detector with us

to the church, strap the battery pack
and headphones on Carolann,

and wait beside the hole. Tonight
the full moon glows like a piece of

pirate gold. We don't even need
our flashlights. And the sound coming

through the instrument is so loud,
we don't even need to ask her

what she hears. Carolann unstraps the
battery pack and goes to stand watch.

I start to tell Malcolm what I think:
We'll need a hacksaw (at least)

to cut through these roots and maybe
something even stronger to blast

through that shale. . . . But I don't
finish. Instead, I stand safely back

from Malcolm—my quiet, introspective friend—
who is already thrusting his shovel

against both of these things, cursing
like a drunken pirate, digging like

Dixon's life depended on it.

SHIFTING SANDS

We dig almost every night this week.
Sometimes one of us stays home
for extra sleep.

On Friday, the three of us meet.
Malcolm brings the measuring tape.
After all this time, the hole is still less than
three
    feet
        deep,
and still no sign of treasure.

Carolann shines her flashlight over
my shoulder while Malcolm and I poke,
with a pair of birch branches,
the few places at the bottom
that aren't covered in shale or tangled in roots.

We find only one spot
where the dirt seems soft and easy to remove.
I lie flat on my belly, reach in and scoop
handfuls of sandy soil, place them on top
of the layer of shale, until

all three of us see, clear as that last full moon,
the outline of a mermaid
engraved on a band of iron.

SHOVEL SHOCK

Nothing could have prepared us
for this.
Nothing anyone could have said
or done
could have prepared us for

this long-haired, fish-tailed lady
engraved in iron
at the bottom of a big pit of dirt
that we've been digging by hand
for almost six weeks.

Anyone spying on us
would see three zombies.
We look like the cartoon character Wile E. Coyote
in that long, long minute
after he's hit by some rocket,
but just before he falls into the canyon, that long, long minute
when he's still as a stone but knows he's going
down.

We've been digging now for so long
without finding anything
that digging, digging, digging, and not finding
anything
has become normal.

Now that we've actually found
something
that looks like the top of a treasure chest,
something
that looks like it might actually be the booty
lost by Captain Kidd
at the
bottom
of the Mullica River
sometime
in the early summer
of 1699,
now that we have actually *found* that . . .

what should we do?

ANALYSIS PARALYSIS

At nine o'clock the next morning
we meet at the church.
Nobody has slept. We don't say much.

Carolann paces the sidewalk awhile,
then reads her new Nancy Drew.
Malcolm hums some blues tunes

and tosses rocks across the parking lot.
I try aiming my kaleidoscope
at the stained glass windows, but it doesn't
look any different unless the sun shines right
into them. The truth is,

we are afraid to go back and look at the hole
we left there late last night,
carefully covered in loose dirt, plastic,
and leafy branches
and protected with the fallen tree,
the hole with the mermaid carved in iron
at the bottom.

We stay there all morning.
Finally, I say: "OK. We have to get
a grip on this . . . we found something, but it's
stuck under a lot of rocks and roots
we can't move. So . . . let's meet tonight at eight-forty-five
in Carolann's family's van,
and let's make a plan."

We stagger separately to our homes.

I lie down on my bed,
point my kaleidoscope at the ceiling light,
watch the patterns scatter, the pieces
slide apart and come back together
in ways I hadn't noticed before.

Part 7

When the moon is in the Seventh House
And Jupiter aligns with Mars,
Then peace will guide the planets
And love will steer the stars.

—from "Aquarius/Let the Sunshine In"
by James Rado, Gerome Ragni, and Galt MacDermot

AUGUST 25, 1968

This would have been my parents'
twentieth wedding anniversary.

Instead, Dad is working late at Glassboro State
grading freshman equations,
and my mother is somewhere
in her new life,
which is somewhere she doesn't want us to know.

Feeling sorry for myself, I eat three
bowls of Cap'n Crunch cereal (the free
"surprise inside" is a tiny plastic treasure chest;
I am not amused) and watch the Phillies
play the Atlanta Braves on NBC.

Outside on the porch,
Denise and Harry are talking and smoking.
When Denise leaves for her evening shift
and Harry for his peace-rally meeting
in Princeton,
I shut off the TV (my mood has improved: the Phillies

are winning in the seventh inning)
and head across the street.

The VW van is gone. "My mom took it to a meeting
in Dennisville," Carolann explains.
She points toward the house. "And Dad
has his buddies over to watch the game."

The evening air is sticky. Big drops begin to hit
the sidewalk like they do just before
a summer downpour.

Malcolm arrives on his bike.
"You OK with going to the diner?" I ask him.
The rain falls harder now.
"It's cheap and close by, and we can use the jukebox
in the booth to cover our talk
about the treasure," I tell him.
(Denise, I'm hoping, will be too busy waiting tables
to bother us. And Mr. Archer
won't even be there.)
Malcolm looks up the street
as if he could see the diner from here.
He nods reluctantly. "Yeah. I guess so. . . ."

Carolann sits on the handlebars of his bike.
I jog alongside.

Eight minutes later we are at the front
door of the Willowbank Diner
being greeted by Mr. Archer himself. *Great.*

"Hi, Boss," I say as cheerfully and politely as I can,
anticipating his reaction
to Malcolm.
"A booth in the back for three, please."

Outside, it's raining in sheets. Thunder claps, rolls.
A family with two kids and a baby bursts in
from the street, squeezing behind us.
Mr. Archer glares at me from the podium.
He shuffles the pile of menus,
deciding what he'll do.

We stand there, dripping wet, waiting.
My lips are still warped in a grin,
but my hands are sweaty,
my stomach knotted up tight.

Malcolm tugs on my sleeve. I ignore him.
If Mr. Archer is a bigot, he'll have to
go public with it, here and now.

Finally, he puts the menus down.
Jeez . . . He really *IS* going to turn
three kids out in the pouring rain . . . just because
one of us is black!

A brown-skirted waitress with an apron
moves between us and Mr. Archer.
"I got these three, Boss," she says efficiently,
grabbing up menus from his podium
and urging us quickly
down the aisle between tables.

We follow her to the booth
in the farthest-back corner of the diner.
Except for the whap-whapping of the kitchen door
when it closes and opens again,
it's quiet, private—
away from eavesdroppers and disapproving eyes.

Malcolm and Carolann slide in
one side, I slide in the other.
The waitress hands us each a menu.

"Thanks, Denise," I say, completely stunned
by what she's just done. She hands me
a towel from her apron. "You three look like wet rats. . . ."
We pass it around, drying our arms and faces.
Denise waves her notepad in the air
and turns toward the front
of the diner. "I'll come back for your orders
in just a minute," she calls over her shoulder.

"I thought you said she's always getting you
into trouble," Malcolm says, his voice shaky
from our Mr. Archer encounter.

"She was . . . *is* . . . *DOES* . . . ," I reply.
"This is definitely strange behavior
for my sister. . . ."

Malcolm folds the towel, pushes it across
the table. "Well, guess what?" His voice is firmer now.
"Your sister's 'strange behavior'
just got me a seat in this diner
for the first time ever."

We celebrate. We order a Triple Suicide Sundae
(five kinds of ice cream, six toppings, nuts,
extra whipped cream) and four spoons.
Despite my objection,
Malcolm insists that Denise should sneak
back to our booth on her break
to share it.

INSPIRATION, PLEASE!

After Denise helps us eat
way too much ice cream, she goes back to waiting
tables out front. Overdosed on sugar, we put
some nickels in the jukebox and listen to Otis Redding,
Steppenwolf, and the Rascals while we try to decide
what to do about the chest.

Carolann does most of the talking:
"None of us are very good with tools,
besides shovels, that is. . . .
And even if we *did* have something
to cut through the roots,
to blast through that shale,
how would we do that and not
destroy
whatever is really down there?"

Carolann, I believe, reads
too many mysteries. But in this case, I think she's right.

So does Malcolm. "If Dixon were here,
we could ask him to help. He could get special saws
and other stuff for us
from the lumberyard. He might not even ask
why we need it. . . ."
His voice trails off. "But anyway, he's *not* here. . . ."

Someone drops a plate in the kitchen.
There's shouting and cursing. A busboy
hurries past.

I fold
and refold my napkin
into something that looks like
a tricornered pirate's hat,
which I place gently on Malcolm's head.

He grins. "What's that?"

"It's your thinking cap. You knew
what the brass key was to
and what the metal detector was for. . . .
I figure if we encourage your brain
just a little bit more,
you'll figure out what we should do
to free that treasure."

THREE BELLYACHES, NO PLAN

We stay at the diner till almost
eleven, kicking around ideas for

raising the chest. First Malcolm suggests
some sort of pulley, made of thick rope

and a kind of hand-cranked crane.
While on the juke, Otis Redding sings,

"Sittin' on the dock o' the bay, wastin' time . . . ,"
Malcolm draws his vision of a homemade

winching system on half a napkin.
"I'm thinkin' that maybe the force of it

lifting might break through those roots
and that shale—and then we wouldn't need

to dig down from the top with any heavy-
duty tools." For a few minutes, we are

convinced. Then Carolann asks, "OK,
but how—exactly—do we get the ropes

underneath the chest in the first place?"
Malcolm sighs. He reaches across the

table and puts the napkin pirate hat
on Carolann. "Your turn—my brain's

tired!" I get up to call Dad on the
pay phone. "I'm fine . . . I'm at the diner,

and Denise is watching me like a hawk,"
I assure him. On the way back

to our booth, I pass the employee
bulletin board, where we thumbtack

messages about switching shifts and
reminders for the busboys and the cooks.

The line of little magnets stuck
around the metal edge gives me an idea.

"How about a giant magnet?" I propose when I
sit down again. "Maybe we could find one

that's strong enough to pull on the metal
parts and—if we're lucky—we can lift it

out of there without wrecking it."
My friends consider this. "It'd have to be

a really, really, *really* big magnet," Carolann
declares. "That chest is *old*, so even if it's not

full of silver and gold, it's probably heavier
than you are." She's right again, of course.

(Jeez, I hate that. I feel like maybe I
need to read more mysteries. . . .)

Another hour passes. We order a piece
of cheesecake and split it three ways.

We draw on napkins, discuss options:
flood the hole, burn the tree roots with

a torch, find a chemical that dissolves
rock but won't harm the chest.

All of them seem possible at first, and then . . .
all of them, it's clear, won't work.

We decide to try again tomorrow night:
meeting site to be determined, cheesecake optional.

SOMETIMES I AM STUPID

"My uncle's invited us up to his cabin
in the Poconos—for three days."
This is Carolann on the phone
the next morning. "I tried to get out of it, but Mom got
mad, so now I *have* to go. We leave after lunch.
You two won't do anything about the . . . *you know* . . .
without me, right?"

I stretch the telephone cord across the kitchen
so I can flip our calendar to September
and the cold reality
of school.

" 'Course not!" I hear myself answer. But there's another,
louder voice in my head that says
we've been lucky so far. In a small town like this,
with the chest exposed in a hole that's
not too far from a church—
how much longer can we leave it there before
someone else finds it?

I hang up with Carolann. I call Malcolm.
"Hey," he whispers into the phone.
"I got some bad news—"

"Oh, swell," I say, cutting Malcolm off.
"I was calling to tell *you* some . . ."

And suddenly I stop my stupid sentence
about Carolann's family going to the Poconos and who knows
when or if we'll get that wooden chest
free and out of that hole.
I stop saying anything about that because right then
I remember about Vietnam.
I remember about Dixon.

My heart pounding, I wait for Malcolm to say something—
anything—
back to me.

LOCAL TROOPS

"My dad's letting the Boy Scouts
use the A.M.E. Church for their troop meetings
for the rest of the year" is what I hear
Malcolm say on the other end.
My heartbeat goes back to normal.

"Oh!" I say, relieved it's nothing serious. Nothing
that involves someone leaving
or someone dead.

"Yeah, but get *this*: Dad also said they could hold
their end-of-the-summer campout
in the woods behind the church."

There goes my heart again—*thump-thump-thump*.
I wonder if you can have a heart attack
before you even start high school.

"When would that be, exactly?" I manage to whisper back.

Malcolm replies: "The weekend after Labor Day."

On the calendar, I put my finger on Labor Day and slide it
over to the next weekend. We have less
than two weeks to get
that chest.

AIRMAIL 2

This afternoon, Malcolm shows up at the diner.
Mr. Archer is not around, so I let Malcolm in
the back, through the kitchen,
and we sit inside the stockroom
to read the letter he just received from Dixon.

Dear Malcolm,

Well, things sure have changed a lot since that first time I wrote. If this is hard to read, it's because I'm writing it with my left hand on account of my right one being in a sling. It's just sprained, though . . . from dragging one of our guys through the mud to his bunker after he got shot by a sniper (bullet caught him in the thigh, but Doc took it out, says he'll be up and walking around again soon).

You could say I've been one of the lucky ones. Since we got sent out here to secure this hill (I figure we're about a hundred miles northeast of Saigon), we've lost two of our guys to sniper fire and four more when they went out on night patrol and met up with an ambush. Then yesterday our gunny sergeant got hit in the gut. It looked pretty bad, too. I sat with him until the chopper came in and got him, took him back to the base. His name is Mike but we all call him Slim because he's about six-foot-four, one hundred thirty pounds. Anyhow, Slim is one of our most experienced soldiers and one of our best shots, so I asked the captain who'd replace him. "Oh, Slim'll be back in a few days. . . . They'll slap some bandages on him, load him up with drugs, and fly him on back here." So, little brother, since it looks like you have to be dead—or almost—to go home, and I plan on staying alive, I guess I'm going to be over here for a while.

The land and the weather in South Vietnam are

weird. Nothing like South Jersey. It rains a lot and there's always some fog around. The swamps are huge and the mosquitoes swarm over them in these big, noisy clouds. The jungle's so thick, you wouldn't think you could walk through it (but somehow we do).

When we're not digging our bunkers, standing a watch, or slinking through the brush on patrol, we try to keep each other laughing as much as possible. We tell jokes, trade food from packages back home—tell Mom to send more peanut butter!—and talk about our families. And here, you find out real quick it doesn't matter where you're from, how old you are, how much money you've got, or what color your skin is (besides me, there's three other blacks in our platoon and one Navajo Indian). Over here, if you don't watch out for the guy next to you, just like he was your own brother, then he's not gonna watch out for you. And since we all know how that ends up, we all treat each other right.

I gotta go now . . . my arm's tired and I'm gonna try and get some shut-eye before my watch. Hug Mom and Dad for me . . . and stay out of trouble. And by the way, how are those Phillies doing? I miss watching the games with you. . . . I miss reading the box scores and tossing the baseball around in the backyard. I miss Fudgsicles and fishing in the Mullica. I miss you all so much. Be good, little brother.

Love,
Dixon

We read the letter together twice.
Then we each read it to ourselves while
the other one waits.
After that, Malcolm says: "You know, I can still
hear his voice
but I'm starting to be afraid I will
forget his face."

"You won't," I tell him.

"How do you know?" he asks. I think of
the two of them—laughing on their porch, tossing
a ball in the yard, fishing side by side
on the bank of the river.
I think of my mom, who's been gone much longer
than Dixon, and how I can still picture her
so clearly.

"I just do," I say.

He's quiet for a minute.
"I think I need to take a walk," he says.

I let him out the back, watch him pass
through the alley and turn onto the street,
a leaner, lankier copy
of his brother.

SUMMER READING

My mathematical dad is at the end of his
summer semester,
which means he's home tonight
correcting tests and typing up final exams
to give to his students. But every once in a while,
I'll catch him watching me
out of the corner of his eye,
making sure I'm doing my chores or reading
something that's on the Summer-Reading List
for freshmen entering Willowbank High.

I would be much more cool with school
if most of it were like this: choosing books
from four different categories (Historical Novels, Biography,
Adventure, Mystery), reading them through,
looking up new vocabulary words,
and writing up short reviews.
Of course for my adventure book,
I chose *Treasure Island*, written by Robert Louis Stevenson
and illustrated by N. C. Wyeth.

Aside from the fact that the story is *relevant*
(one of my vocabulary words—it means "related; having
a logical connection") to my life right now
and is one of the best things I've ever read,
I end up spending half the time
staring at the amazing illustrations of Long John Silver,

Billy Bones, and Ben Gunn, trying to imagine
what it must have been like
to be a pirate—a man
(or a woman, I guess, according to Carolann)
who sailed to Africa, India, and the Caribbean,
risking his life for silver, gold, and precious jewels,
living only by his own pirate rules.

"Nice to see you enjoying your summer reading," Dad says.
I twitch in surprise at his interruption.
I don't want to seem *too* interested
or Dad might get suspicious.

"Yeah," I say, as casually as possible.
"Who knew the classics were so fascinating?!"
I close the book, yawn, toss it onto the coffee table.
"A little far-fetched, though, ya know. All those
pirates and treasure and stuff. . . ."

But I don't need to bluff.
Dad has gone back to correcting tests
and he doesn't even hear me.

NOT SLEEPING TOO WELL MYSELF

I have nightmares
of Long John Silver,
the blind pirate Pew,
and a few of the others
from the *Treasure Island*
crew, stumbling through
the dark across the
churchyard and
back through the trees,
finding our
hand-dug hole,
our mermaid
engraved in iron
at the bottom, then
stealing our treasure
and running off
down the path
beside the river.
In my dream,
we never find them.

DAYDREAM BELIEVER

All day at work I keep having
a waking version of my nightmare:
someone finding the chest before we have a chance
to raise it up, see what's inside.
I phone Malcolm at noon to tell him I'm worried,
but no one's there.

Later, when I get home from the diner, there's a note
from Dad: *Giving exams tonight. Be home late.*
Call my office if you need anything.

I leap onto my bike, pedal over to the church, and just keep
circling, circling, circling—
like a vulture over a rabbit carcass—
around and around the parking lot
so I can keep watch, at least from a distance,
on our digging spot.

It's getting dark earlier now
and there's a coolness to the breeze
that makes me think of marching bands and football.
I stop my bike for a minute under one of the big oak trees.
I look up at the steeple of the A.M.E. Church
and as I'm saying a little silent prayer
for Dixon, stuck in the jungles of Vietnam
(*please, God, don't let him get shot*),
and for our chest (*please, please, don't let*
anyone get to it before we do),

and for my mom (*please watch over her,*
wherever she is),
a stream of green-shirted Boy Scouts pours out of the front doors
and down the steps,
fanning out in twos and threes to the bicycle rack
or to the sidewalk leading back
to Main Street.

Johnny Fetterline is there.
I had a serious crush on him last year,
until I heard he'd been dating Darleen Hummel,
who has the largest chest of any girl in our class
and the IQ of a Tootsie Roll.
(So much for Johnny F.)

None of them sees me tucked back here
behind the big oak in the far corner
of the lot. A red Chevy with a blond-haired driver
who looks kind of familiar
cruises slowly by. It hesitates, then guns away.

I wait there until even the Scout leader
leaves in his dusty tan Rambler
and the whole place is still and quiet, empty.

I consider going back to our hole,
to be sure everything's just how we left it.
But then I decide against it: too risky
with no one standing watch.

I circle the parking lot one last time
before heading home.

UNDER SUSPICION

"You getting religious all of a sudden?"
That is Denise's question
the next morning while I'm prying
the *third* burned English muffin
out of the toaster. I have no idea what English
muffins have to do with religion.

I hold the fork with the black disk on it
up to Denise's face
so she can see how really bad we need
to talk to Dad about home improvements.
"You'd think with the three of us working all the time,
we could afford a new toaster," I say,
still ignoring her question.

"Suzi saw you hangin' out at the A.M.E. Church
last night," she says. "And I know why."

OK. *Now* Denise has my complete attention.
I force my own face to read

blank. I turn quick
back to the toaster and pretend to be fishing out
more pieces of muffin.
My palms get sweaty. I wonder
if I will electrocute myself right here in the kitchen.

I unplug the machine and turn it upside
down so a thousand toasted bread crumbs spill onto the counter.
My mind goes into overdrive.
That was Suzi in the red Chevy.
But she couldn't know about the treasure, could she?
Think, Lyza, think.
I didn't go back to the woods last night. . . .
But could Suzi—or Denise—have seen us back there
some other time when we thought we were alone?

"Oh, really?" I ask her over my shoulder
easy and casual, like I don't even care.
"Why is that?"

Denise saunters over to me, hands on her hips,
clearly enjoying whatever it is she's
found out about me, which is something
I can't prevent now. I suck in my breath.
She pokes my left shoulder with her index finger.

"Admit it, Lyza . . . you still have a crush
on Johnny Fetterline," she announces triumphantly.

I take a few seconds
to let that misinformation sink in.
I look down at my feet so she
can't see my relief.
It's scary to think that at one time
Denise had plans to go to medical school.

REUNITED

As soon as Carolann gets
back from her uncle's cabin in the Poconos,
she calls me: "I've got to watch the twins
all afternoon,
but we can meet tonight in our van. . . ."

My dad is home again this evening, correcting exams
and paying down the mountain of bills
that have been piling up on his desk all summer.
I decide it's better
to ask his permission to go across the street
than to sneak. "Hey, Dad . . . ," I say, peering over
his shoulder at the bills for ladies' clothes and shoes,
others for framing supplies, and a few bold-print
collection notices stamped in blue: *Past Due*.

I change my question. "Whose are those?" I ask.
Denise and I don't buy clothes
and shoes at those stores. . . .

Dad puts down his pen. He takes off his reading glasses.
He runs his hand several times
through his hair. "They're left over
from your mother, Lyza. You remember how we never
could agree about money?" I nod. (Yep, I sure do remember that.)
"Well, your mom was spending a lot more money
than we were making before she left—
and now that she's gone, I'm trying to get rid of
all this debt." He spreads his hands out wide
over the desk, covered in envelopes and bills and a few
random math tests.

"Oh," I say, trying to let my brain take this in.
I look down at the dozen or so torn-
open envelopes, the collection notices spread across the desk,
which now seem like maps
to our family's self-destruction.
I knew my parents fought a lot about money. But I didn't know
we were still in debt because of it.
I guess that explains Dad's teaching extra classes, our broken-
down house and kitchen gadgets.

I rest my hand on Dad's shoulder. He reaches up
with his hand and puts it on top of mine.
"I'm sorry, Lyza."

"For what?" I ask.

"For not being around very much these last couple of years."
He means it, I can tell. And suddenly his saying it
means a lot to me, too.
"That's OK," I say, trying to keep things light. "We don't
miss you *that* much. . . ." I laugh and he does, too,
and I realize his laughter is something
I *have* missed.

The hall clock chimes seven.
"Dad—can I go over to Carolann's? Just till nine."

He shifts in his chair so he can see through the front
window, across the street to where
Mr. Mott is working in the yard (Dad must still be
a little worried about me).
He squeezes my hand, releases it.
"Sure," he says. "Stay as late as you want.
It won't be too long now and you'll be doing
homework at night."

"I know," I reply, already halfway to the door.
"Don't remind me!"

SWEET-TALKIN'

Malcolm and Carolann are already inside the van
eating Mt. Pocono peanut brittle
from a bright orange can.
"OK," I say. "Let's get started. We have to
come out of here tonight
with a plan for getting that chest."

Malcolm agrees. "Once those Boy Scouts start
tromping around in the woods,
they're gonna find it."

"Unless we fill the hole back in," Carolann offers, breaking
off a huge piece of brittle, splitting it
in two, handing a half
                                   each to Malcolm and me.

"But then what?" Malcolm points out. "We're right
back where we are now. Plus we're in school,
which complicates everything
and takes up a whole lot of time."

We go back over all the ideas we had
that night at the diner:
1. Flood the hole to soften the roots
   (won't do much to break up the rock).
2. Use acid to dissolve the shale and use tools
   to cut through the roots (the acid might destroy the chest
   and whatever's in it; we don't have the right tools).

3. Burn the roots with a torch
   (ditto—too risky for the chest).
4. Use ropes and a pulley to lift it up from underneath
   (but how do we *get* the ropes under the chest in the first
   place?).

We eat way too much peanut brittle, hoping a little
sugar high will provide the answer.

It doesn't.

Finally, I say what I've been thinking about
for the past three days: "Guys . . .
I think I know a way that might work."

My friends stop chewing. I wait.
"Well, OK already," Carolann says, gulping down
what's in her mouth and putting the lid on the can.
"Let's hear it."

I am quiet a minute, as if silence
might help me believe that my idea
is the right one, the one that Gramps himself
would choose if he were alive, if he were in charge of
this adventure,
    this problem,
       this chest,
          this mess,
this three-foot-deep hole with tree roots and shale,

with an iron band and a mermaid,
with green-shirted Boy Scouts,
with hardly any time left
till school.

I take a deep breath.
"I think we need to tell Harry."

OFF THE RECORD

After work on Tuesday, I ride my bike
two miles over to the lumberyard
and wait.

At five-thirty, Harry walks across the parking lot toward
his car,
where I am drawing circles in the gravel
with my sandal.

"Hey, Lyza—what's going on?"
He's definitely not expecting to see me way out here.

Then, quickly, a little desperately: "Is Denise OK?"
(Jeez, he even *sounds* like a husband!)

"Oh, yeah. She's fine," I reassure him.
"Probably home burning another meat loaf right now."

He laughs as he unlocks his trunk,
pulls off his gray Dillard's Lumber T-shirt,
exchanging it for another one with a caricature
of Paul McCartney on the front.
Harry's chest is tan, his shoulders stronger
than I imagined. One thing's for sure:
Denise has much better taste in men
than in music.

I look around to be sure we're alone.
"Harry?" My voice isn't too steady.

He looks at me more seriously now.
His right hand slams the trunk shut.
"What is it?"

"Harry . . . I need to know if you can keep
a secret."

His eyes narrow just a bit. He looks at me funny.
"Lyza, does this secret have anything to do
with Denise—or with anything illegal?"

I shake my head. "No . . . it's not about Denise.
Honest. I would tell you. And I am NOT
buying, selling, or using *any drugs*!"

Harry studies me. He jingles his car keys.
"OK. Yeah. I've kept my share
of secrets for people. So what's yours?"

I lift my bike off the ground, swing my right leg over.
"Meet me in the parking lot of the
A.M.E. Church. I'll get there quick as I can."

Harry's not with me—yet.
"Why? What's up at the church?"

"Please. Just . . . just *trust* me. I promise
I'll explain everything once we're there."

I start pedaling away, not wanting to give him
any more time to decide.
I turn onto the main road and pick up speed.
It feels good, for a change, to use my legs
instead of my back and shoulders.

As Harry passes me,
I can hear John, Paul, George, and Ringo
singing "A Hard Day's Night" on the radio,
which, come to think of it,
sums up the whole summer
pretty darn well.

ANOTHER KIND OF COMMUNION

My friends are sitting on the front steps
talking to Harry when I arrive.
Carolann has the maps

and the handwritten transcript
of Captain Kidd's ship's log;
Malcolm has the key to get us into

the church. We enter by the back door,
walk through the kitchen, and spread the maps across
the choir-room floor.

Malcolm turns on the light that's over
the piano, and the three of us sit
on the bench. Harry sits cross-legged on

the floor, looking confused but, so far,
patient. Since we're in church, I pray
silently that I have not misjudged him—

that he will keep our secret
and not rat us out. And more important,
that he'll actually help us.

After we agreed that Harry might be
our only answer to saving the chest,
we decided that each of us should

tell one part of our story, and since
Harry knows me the best of the three,
I got elected to start. First I explain how

I found the maps and the letter
from Gramps; then Malcolm reads
the documents we found in Brigantine;

then Carolann tells how we used all that,
plus the metal detector, to find the site
we've been digging up at night

right behind the church. "We don't
come every night—just as often
as we can," she explains, sliding off

the bench, pacing a little, then sitting
back down again. "Sometimes it's just
two of us, sometimes all three,

but we've been sneaking over here
for more than six weeks and now we're
stuck." When Carolann's done,

Harry stands. He looks down at the
maps and then at the three of us
lined up on the piano bench like

magpies on a fence. Finally, he says:
"That story is so wild . . . you can't
possibly be making it up."

I feel all three of us breathe
a sigh of relief. He believes us!
"So when do I get to see . . . ?"

A wedge of light sprawls across
the choir-room floor. "Someone's comin'—
grab the maps!" Malcolm croaks.

We dive down and gather them up.
Malcolm tucks them in his shirt.
And Harry—color-blind, grave-keeping,

Denise-loving Harry—stands
like a soldier between us
and whoever has intruded.

IMPROVISATION

The wedge of light
that sprawled across the choir-room floor
is quickly blocked by the full figure
of Mrs. Eunice Carter.

"Malcolm DuPREEEE!" she bellows.
Her eyes slide across the rest of us.
"What are you-all *doin'* in here?"

Sweat beads are already popping out across
Malcolm's forehead. "Aunt Eunice! . . . uh . . .
hi . . . uh . . . we were just . . . uh . . ."

Stepping toward her, Harry interrupts.
"Excuse me, ma'am—uh, Mrs. Carter . . .
you see, I was just . . . uh . . . I don't have
a piano at home and I was just . . . uh . . .
hoping to use this one here to . . . umm . . .
to rehearse a Beatles tune."

Mrs. Carter's eyes light up. "Oh, I *love* them.
Which one you singin'?"

I exchange looks with Carolann:
Uh-oh. He'd better pick one we
all know the words to.

Harry turns around, starts walking slowly toward
the piano. He looks at me, mouthing:
"Ticket to Ride"? and I nod *OK*.

We gather around the piano
with Harry playing,
Malcolm and me singing alto,
Carolann and Mrs. Carter singing soprano,
and we belt out the most
unrehearsed, improvised version of "Ticket to Ride"
that South Jersey has ever heard.

UNVEILING

After singing that song with us twice more,
Aunt Eunice leaves with her sheet music
and her casserole dish
(which is what she came there for).

We wait, just to be safe, in the parking lot
in Harry's car
until the sun goes down, until we're sure
no one else is around. Malcolm stands watch

while Carolann and I take Harry through the side yard,
which we've walked across
so many times that we know it by heart
even in the moonless dark.

At the woods' edge, I flick on my flashlight,
let the beam fall
on the tree trunk about ten feet in.
"There—can you see anything?" I ask.

Harry peers into the woods. He shakes
his head. "Nope. Not a thing."
Carolann and I smile. "Good," she says. "Because we spent
almost as much time covering this thing
as we did trying to dig it up!"

We roll back the tree, lift the branches
and the plastic. We lie on our bellies, scoop
out a few shoefuls of loose dirt. We move
away so Harry can look down
into the hole at the long-haired,
fish-tailed woman at the bottom.

FEMININE PERSUASION

Harry just keeps repeating:
"Man . . . unbelievable. Man oh
man oh man . . . unbelievable. . . . *Man*."

And then: "You did all this yourselves, by *hand?*"
We show him our bruised wrists
and blistered fingers.
We show him the hollow tree where we've been dumping
most of the dirt.

He walks around the hole. He pulls
on his ponytail. Then he walks around again, staring
down at the mermaid and the tangle of tree roots
that have grown around the chest
like an octopus clinging to a boat.
He pokes the shelf of shale with a branch;
he lies down, removes his boot, and pounds it
with the heel. "That's not budging."

"We know," I say. "And that's why we need
your help. We need special tools and someone who's
strong enough to use them
to break through the rock and the roots."

Carolann pulls one of her mystery books
from her knapsack: *The Mystery of the Fire Dragon*.
On the cover, it shows a man
using a pointed thing with a handle

to smash the thick rock wall
of his cell.

"How about something like this?" she asks,
holding the book up to Harry's face.

"That's a pickax," Harry explains.
"We have some at Dillard's. . . ." He leans over
the center of the hole.
"Yeah, a pickax might do the trick.
Probably a hacksaw and lopping shears for the roots."

He turns to me:
"Your father knows nothing about this?"
     "Nope," I reply.
"How about Denise?"
     "Nope."

He nods toward Carolann and back to Malcolm.
"Not their parents, either?"
     "*Uh-uh.*"

"Nobody but you three?"
     "Nope—just you. And you *promised*," I remind him.

Harry holds up his hand.
"I know, I know. Don't sweat it, Lyza. . . .
It's just . . . well, we *use* the tools at the lumberyard
during the day—"

"But not at night, right?" I interrupt. "No one would
know if we borrowed them then—right?"

"No, not at night. Yard's closed till morning."

"Perfect!" I say. "Then can you bring them here
on Thursday after work? We'll meet you
at eight-forty-five."

I stand on one side of the hole.
Harry stands on the other. I look him straight in the face
and wait for his reply.

At last he sighs, shakes his head.
"Good Lord! How did I end up taking orders from
two Bradley women?"

Part 8

Lately things just don't seem the same.
Actin' funny, but I don't know why. . . .

—from "Purple Haze"

by Jimi Hendrix

LATE-SUMMER STATS

10,000: Estimated number of anti-war protesters at the
      Democratic National Convention in Chicago.

12,000: Estimated number of police—same place.

6,000: Number of National Guardsmen called in as
      reinforcements.

7,500: Number of U.S. Army troops called to Chicago
      to help quiet the riots.

And all this time
we thought
the war
was in Vietnam.

AMBITIOUS

Wednesday passes pretty quickly.
Thursday is an eternity. On my work shift, I triple-wash
every glass and dish. I stack and restack
the dinner plates, rearrange the bowls.
Mary Sue glares at me the whole time.
"Don't be so ambitious," she scolds.
"Makes the rest of us look lazy."
That wouldn't be hard, I feel like saying. (But I don't.)

At home, I heat up the least-burned piece
of Denise's meat loaf and choke it down.
I sweep the kitchen and vacuum every room.
Dad calls home at precisely eight-thirty.
"I'm giving my last exam, so don't wait up.
But leave the lights on, OK?"

OK, Dad.   No problem.   Click.   Breathe.

Carolann and Malcolm are outside waiting.
They look as nervous as I feel.

"We should split up tonight," Carolann suggests.
"Take different ways to the church. Just in case."

This seems like spillover from her mystery-book reading.
I turn to Malcolm. "Can't hurt," he shrugs.

"OK," I say. "I'll take Maple—you two take Walnut or Main."

We head out separately. We meet up again shortly
in the churchyard, where Harry Keating
promised he'd be waiting,
but he is nowhere to be found.

SLIVER

We sit together
    at the edge of
        the A.M.E. Church
           parking lot waiting
              under the starry
          sky with the thin
        sliver of moon: five, ten,
    fifteen, twenty minutes—
and still, no sign of Harry.

DON'T LOOK N.O.W.

A pair of headlights spear the dark
and we are deer
caught by flashlight in the neighbor's garden.
I have seen
the look on Denise's face when Harry is late
and I have
that same look now as Harry kills the engine
and jumps out.
Dressed entirely in black, he is carrying
a canteen.
"Sorry, guys," he says. "The boss had a meeting
after closing
and I couldn't get the tools until everyone left."
He pops open
the trunk, pulls out a pickax, hands Malcolm
the hacksaw and shears.
"I know the National Organization for Women wouldn't approve,
but I'm only
willing to do this *once*," Harry says. "So how 'bout
us guys give this
our best shot while you girls stand watch?" Malcolm—
who at first was mad
at God *and* at Harry (for not getting drafted)—now
seems to like
having Harry around. "Good idea," he says. But
Carolann frowns.
"That's not real fair to us, ya know. . . ." She wags

her index finger,
looking to me for support. Truthfully, I am torn:
I think of all
those pictures of protesting women in Denise's
feminist newsletters,
and I'm sure *they* would be pretty miffed about this.
On the other hand,
August is almost over, our backs are sore,
and the chest
will stay stuck unless we get it out of there—tonight.
I decide a small
compromise is in order. "Let's let them try for an hour,"
I propose to Carolann,
"and see what they can do with the tools. Then maybe
we can switch:
we work and they watch." She considers this, then agrees.
I turn back to
the guys. "Is it a deal?" I ask. "Yeah, cool," Harry says.
"I'll whistle if we
break through," Malcolm adds. We hand them our flashlights
and they head off toward
the woods—the tall, thin black kid and my sister's strong,
long-haired boyfriend.
Carolann giggles: "They are the most unusual pair of pirates
I've ever seen."

A LITTLE NIGHT MUSIC

I sit on a rock in the side yard
of the A.M.E. Church. Carolann stands

between the back door and the woods,
humming occasionally and slapping

mosquitoes frequently. In the trees,
the locusts and crickets make

their insect racket, which blends in
almost naturally with the percussion

of the pickax pounding shale.

VIGIL

Only four cars have passed by the church
in the last fifty minutes.
The crickets, the katydids, and one stray cat
are our only company
as we wait, listen.

Only once did we hear someone coughing
and then, a little later, what must have been
the SNAP of a root
as it was split by the shears.
In between, there's been the dull *thud*
of the pickax against rock.

I look back at Carolann, who happens to be
looking toward me.
She holds up her wrist, taps her watch.
Ten-fifteen—time to switch.

I begin walking back to Carolann,
back toward the woods,
and that's when we hear Malcolm's low, steady whistle.

FADE TO BLACK

We run so hard, we almost fall into the
hole. We stop just short and I realize

my heart has slid up into my head, where
it's pounding like a snare drum.

My hands feel numb. I am afraid to look
down. Instead, I look at Malcolm

and Harry, who are both drenched in
sweat and breathing hard from a solid

hour of pounding and digging. Carolann
grabs my left hand— "LOOK!"—and when

I do, I see the perfectly preserved
top of a wooden chest with *two* thick

bands of iron, each engraved with a
mermaid, and a smaller metal plate

on which I read the name: *KIDD*.
Then, suddenly, everything goes black.

REALITY CHECK

I am that famous explorer
who found the long-lost tribe
of pygmies and who could not get them
to stop staring.

Squatting in front of me, they study
my every move.

"Are you OK?" I hear one of them say.
Everything's hazy. My back is propped
against a tree and it seems
they've thrown the canteen water on me.
My blue jeans feel wet—yuck.
My shirt feels sticky.

"Did I really faint?" I inquire. (I have never
come close to doing that before.)

"Yeah, you dropped like a brick, Lyza,"
Malcolm says. "You all right now?"

I pinch my wrist. It hurts.
I wiggle my toes and shake out my arms.
"Guess so. . . . Hey, where's Harry?"

TWO BY THREE

My friends are bookends on either
side of me. They tell me to breathe,
even though I know (OK, even though
I'm *pretty sure*) I won't faint again.
While they have been watching over me,
Harry has been clearing away the dirt
and roots from the front of the chest,
which is smaller than I imagined—
maybe three feet long by two feet wide.
Harry lies on his stomach. He reaches
down into the hole, ready to use the
hacksaw to cut the loop of the lock
that holds it closed. He looks up at us.
"Ready?" We inhale, exhale together.
We drop down to our bellies beside
him. "Yeah—no, wait!" I say, grasping
his wrist. "Shouldn't we lift it out of there
first?" Harry looks at Malcolm, Carolann,
then back at me. "That's really up to
you three . . . but if you ask me, I say
leave it. If this chest is really what you
suspect, it's been down in the wet dirt
for more than 250 years . . . you take a
big chance if you try to move it. It could
be all rotten on the bottom and anything
inside might get ruined. But . . . like I
said, it's really up to you." I turn to

Carolann, who, I can see, is already
flipping through the Rolodex of
detective books she has stored inside
her head. "We can always move it
later . . . ," she offers. "If you can
reach it from here, let's open it."
Malcolm nods his agreement. "OK,"
I say to Harry. "Do it!" He slips the
tool underneath the metal loop. Once,
twice, three times he saws before the
loop splits in two. My throat feels funny.
I try to breathe, breathe, breathe.
I think back to my porch dream, the
one with the chest of human bones.
Snap out of it, I tell myself. *This is real—*
this is New Jersey, not Vietnam.
Malcolm nudges me. "You should
open it, Lyza. This all started with you."
Carolann agrees. "Absolutely—
but, jeez, please *hurry up*!"

ANCHOR LEG

"Hold my feet!"

I stretch
   down
      into the
         hole and
            grab the part above the lock,

the two mermaids staring, daring me to go any further.

WHAT LIES BENEATH

I curl my fingers under the thin iron rim
of the chest. I pull up.

It doesn't budge.
My fingers slip off.

"Pull up hard, Lyza," Harry instructs.
"The wood will be warped and there's probably
a lot of dirt in the hinges."

I try again. CRACK! The wood on the top
splits
and I am left holding the front half of the lid.
The back half stays in place.

Inside the chest, everything's covered in
a thin layer of sand and mud.

"Shine the light down here more!" I whisper
over my shoulder.
Carolann adjusts the beam so that it
falls directly on the open half of the chest.

I scrape my palm gently
back and forth across the top
of whatever's in there . . . until
we can see—
glittering in the beam of Carolann's flashlight
and as clear as the crystals in my kaleidoscope—
a layer of gold and silver coins
and two golfball-size gems.

INVERTED

We take turns holding one another's
feet so everyone can lean in
and see.

Carolann can't stop whispering, I can't
stop my lower lip from
quivering—

and Malcolm hasn't smiled this much since
before Dixon left. Harry,
who can't tell

that the gems are different colors, can tell enough
to know that they are something
very special. He just

keeps shaking his head: "Man . . . oh
man oh *man* . . . no one
is gonna

believe this." On his turn, Harry manages
to pry open the back part
of the chest—

behind the coins and gems, there are four
smaller sacks filled with more
gold and silver coins,

two odd-looking brown and white rocks,
and a square container with
some white powder

inside. There's also a metal box of necklaces
and rings and a few large pieces
of mostly

disintegrated cloth. After Harry comes up, I go
down again and find—hidden in some
moldy linen—

a spyglass etched with the initials *W.K.*

ALIBI

"Malcolm *DuPREEEE!*"
I have heard that voice somewhere before.

I am almost done
brushing myself off when we hear it. Malcolm
freezes. "Oh, Lord . . . Aunt *Eunice.*"
He slips behind a tree. "Why is she—"

Carolann interrupts. "It's almost midnight,"
she whispers, holding the beam on her
wristwatch for me and Harry to see.
"Someone noticed we were gone."

Through the trees, we can see Mrs. Carter
and Malcolm's father
walking around the back of the church, swinging
their own flashlights side to side.

Suddenly it's too quiet—even the locusts seem to be sleeping.
Harry speaks first.
"Look," he whispers, "no one has found this out
so far. I think you should keep what you've got
and leave the rest of it down there—
for tonight, anyhow."

Carolann opens her hand. She's holding
several silver coins and a green-stoned ring.
Malcolm steps out. He has a small bag
of gold coins and a chain with a purple stone.
I have one of the weird brown and white rocks,
the red gem, and the spyglass.
Harry has nothing.

Our three pairs of eyes meet in silent agreement.
We pocket our treasure.

Our hands and feet fly to dump in some loose dirt,
branches, the plastic cover, more branches,
and finally the dead tree, rolled back on top.
Harry stashes the tools. "I'll come get them
in a few hours," he whispers.

Meanwhile, Malcolm's father and aunt have started across
the backyard, toward us.
"*This way!*" Harry waves us away from the
dig site, so we come out on the church lawn
about twenty yards down.

"I hope you can steal us an idea
from one of your mysteries," I whisper to Carolann.
"We need an alibi here. . . ."
She looks as panicky as I feel. But then she grins,
points to her head. "I'm on it!"

TALL TALES

We are nearly close enough to see their faces.
Malcolm's dad walks like someone who's really mad.
Carolann grabs me by the arm, pulls me toward

her and Malcolm. *"Hey . . . slow down!"* she mutters.
"Stagger a little. . . ." (Oh, God—now I'll be accused of
drinking, *too*?) But I'm wrong. This time, Carolann's plan

uses honesty; at least it starts out that way: *"Oh—Mr. Dupree,
Mrs. Carter! Thank goodness you've come,"* she exclaims
as I lean against her and Malcolm. *"Lyza fainted and we*

weren't sure we could get her home!" Actually, I still do
feel a little light-headed, so the staggering part isn't hard.
"Poor thing! Look, brother—she's bleeding!" says Aunt Eunice.

Another surprise—I have some dried blood on my forehead.
Malcolm's dad doesn't look so mad now. "Got a call from
Lyza's father . . . then realized you weren't in bed, either,"

he says to Malcolm. Then to us: "What are you all doing
out here at this hour, anyhow?" Malcolm, who's almost allergic
to lying, tries to explain: "Lyza lost something from her family

near here. . . ." He pauses, looks at me. "Maybe during the
picnic or the baseball game. She asked us to help her find it. . . ."
His voice drifts off. Harry steps forward. "Uh—Mr. Dupree—

if you'll excuse me, I think I can explain." We listen as Harry,
who hardly knows us and doesn't owe us anything, explains
how he "happened to drive by" while we were searching in the

churchyard for "Lyza's family keepsake," which I thought
I lost at the picnic, and how important it was to me personally,
and how Malcolm and Carolann had promised to help me,

and how I tripped on a rock in the dark and fainted, and how—
about an hour later—I was just getting back on my feet. Harry
is a good actor. "Mr. Dupree, you have raised a responsible son,"

he says as Malcolm's eyebrows arch way up. "These kids
have stuck together to be sure Lyza's all right, even though
they know they might get into trouble for being out so late. . . ."

Harry pauses for dramatic effect. "Now if you'll both excuse me,
I'd like to take Lyza home to her father and sister."
The adults look totally convinced. Aunt Eunice offers me

a handkerchief for my head. Malcolm's dad helps me over
to Harry's car, where I slide into the back in case I need to lie
down. "Well, Lyza, after all that—did you find it?" he inquires.

I look helplessly at my friends' faces. The last thing we need
is for people to start snooping around the church for my sake.
I make a decision. I reach into my pocket for the odd brown

and white rock. But Malcolm beats me to it. "Here!" he almost
shouts, holding out the chain with the purple stone (which looks
more like something you can buy at the jewelry store).

"You almost forgot!" Malcolm drops it onto my lap and closes Harry's back door. Like I said once before, my family might be messed up, but my friends are as steady as they come.

Part 9

It's been a hard day's night.
I should be sleeping like a log. . . .
—from "A Hard Day's Night"
by John Lennon and Paul McCartney

PROPOSAL

Carolann rides home with Malcolm,
Aunt Eunice, and Mr. Dupree.
Now it's just Harry and me
cruising slowly down Main Street.

He turns, stops, turns again, then pulls
over on Gary Street about half a block from our house.
He kills the engine. We sit, silent.
"Are you mad?" I ask.

He swivels to face me in the backseat.
"Mad? . . . No, no, I guess not."
He scratches his arm, still smeared with dirt.
I can see he's trying hard to get his mind
around all of this—which is exactly what
I'm trying to do, too. Until now, we could simply
follow the maps,
dig when we were able, stay quiet,
and just keep going. But now . . .

I take the brown and white rock
from my pocket, the red gem from my sock,
the spyglass from the waistband
of my blue jeans. I spread them out on the backseat, next to
the necklace from Malcolm.
We stare at them a long time—
at least it *seems* like a long time.

Finally, Harry sighs: "I have a friend—a guy I met
at a protest. He's a professor at Princeton.
I don't know for sure if he'll be able to tell us much
about what you've found. But if he can't,
he'll know someone who can."

I wait for him to continue.

"It's up to you, Lyza.
But if this stuff is what you think it is—
a treasure chest lost by Captain Kidd—
well . . . unless you plan to keep it in your closet
and never say a word about it,
it seems like you should be showing it
to someone
who can tell you for sure what these things are,
what they're actually worth."
He pauses and looks at me, square. Just like Dad did
before that first time we drove
to Tuckahoe. "What you have here
is a significant piece of history. And even though
whatever it's worth might belong to you,

the history of this belongs
to everyone."

I run my finger across the spyglass,
which looks like an antique version of my
kaleidoscope.

"So—you think we should go public?" I ask.

Harry nods. "Yep. I do."

Here we go again . . . another decision. Why are there
so *many* of them? If this were a math equation,
it would look like this:

adventure = problem + problem + problem + problem

I just hope   I choose   the right   solution.

BUTTERFINGERS

That night, I sleep for about ten minutes—total.

I get up at seven. I check to be sure
the spyglass is well hidden

                                    underneath my bed.
I call Malcolm at eight, Carolann at eight-thirty.

I drink two Coca-Colas from the fridge
and run down to the diner.
My caffeine fix lasts until lunch, after which I
drop and break two plates
and one water glass.
I spend almost as much time sweeping up
as I do washing.

Mr. Archer is not forgiving.
"Those come out of your paycheck, Miss Bradley!"
he bellows so the entire kitchen staff
can hear. What a *jerk*.

I watch the clock like a hawk
between four and four-thirty p.m. At 4:31, I fling
my apron into the stockroom, bolt out
the back door, and make straight
for the A.M.E. Church—

where this time, just as he promised,
Harry Keating is waiting.

REPLAY

Malcolm, it turns out, has been walking or riding
his bike up and
                        down the street in front of the church
nearly all day, keeping
a loose watch on the backyard and the woods—
just in case.

Since noon, Carolann
has been
        sitting on the
                church steps
                        reading the same chapter
of *Nancy Drew: The Hidden Staircase*
over and over.

They both come running when they see me.
"Is that him?" Malcolm asks, nodding
toward the parking lot, where Harry is getting
out of his car with someone
we've never seen before.

I shrug. "Guess so—Harry said he'd show
his professor friend those few things that we
grabbed from the chest, then see
if he would come down here."

"But can we *trust* him?" Carolann demands.
Since the beginning, this has been

our million-dollar question. From Gramps to me, from me
to Carolann and Malcolm, from them to Harry,
and now from all of us to—
whoever he is—from Princeton.

I gaze into my friends' tired faces.
"Look at us," I say. "In a week we go back to school.
We're bruised and we're beat
and—I think—we're tired of keeping secrets?"

They don't argue. I take that as a *yes*.
"I spent all last night thinking about this,"
I continue, "about what's best for us, about what
Gramps would want.
And I realized that we will never know if this is
what we *think* it is . . . we'll never find out
what it's worth
or if it's of any use
unless we let an expert see it."

Gravel crunches nearby. Harry and the new guy,
dressed in blue jeans and work boots,
walk toward us across the parking lot.
"Lyza—Carolann—Malcolm," Harry says.
"This is Trent Taylor, from the Archaeology Department
at Princeton."

Professor Taylor shakes our hands.
He has calluses in the same places I do. I like him.

"Trent and I met at a peace rally," Harry continues.
"I've gotten to know him pretty well over
the summer. You three can trust him with this,
same as you did me."

Professor Taylor steps forward, holds out a clear
plastic bag that contains
the red gem, the purple necklace,
and the weird brown and white stone.
"So you three found and dug up *these*?"

I take a deep breath. I glance over at my two
best friends once again. They look exhausted.
As much fun as it was for us to be
treasure hunters,
this project has become too complicated
for us to finish on our own.
I know Gramps would understand.

"Yes, sir," I answer for the three of us.
"And we'd like to show you how. . . ."
I nod toward Malcolm.

"Let's do it," Malcolm says, holding up
the key to the church.

Inside, we spread the maps across the choir-room floor.
Carolann brings out the green-stoned ring

and the silver coins. Malcolm displays
the gold. Then, in front of Professor Taylor,
we replay the day
we first explained everything to Harry.

But this time, we don't
have to sing.

HISTORY LESSON

Professor Taylor stares at us.
He doesn't say anything—
at first.

Then he takes the strange brown and white rock
from the plastic bag
and holds it up.
"This is a bezoar stone. Back in my lab,
I dated it around the mid-1600s.
It's from India and was made from the intestines
of a sacred goat. Back then, people believed it had
miraculous healing powers. Captain Kidd
probably kept it in case he needed
an antidote—for poison."

He pauses, puts it down. His voice is calm
but when he takes out the red gem,
his hands tremble.
"This . . . is an African ruby. I'm not sure yet
about the year, but you can bet
if we were able to turn this into cash,
you three could buy a few blocks of houses
in this town."

He lifts the purple necklace, his hands still shaking.
"Amethyst. Probably from South America.
Polished and set like this,
and off a seventeenth-century ship,
I'd guess it's worth almost as much as the ruby"—
he nods toward the green ring—"or that emerald.
The coins I'd need to clean and date,
but from here they appear to be
English gold and Spanish silver."

He gets quiet again.

Beside me, Carolann jiggles both feet.
Malcolm sweats.
I realize I am opening and closing my hands
butterfly-style,
just like my dad. My stomach churns.

"We'd like a few minutes to talk things over
between us," I hear myself say.

Harry takes Professor Taylor
back outside.

Malcolm, Carolann, and I
fold up the maps, place the coins and gems
into the plastic bag, carry them
over to the table behind the piano.
I take out the list I scribbled today
during my break at the diner.
I place the paper in the center
so we all can read it.
I give Carolann a red pen, Malcolm a blue one.
"Write down anything else you can think of," I tell them.

And they do.

PROS AND CONS

At the top of the paper, I have written this:
Should we go public with our treasure?
Below that question, I have drawn
a horizontal line across the middle.

Then I've listed the reasons why we *should*,
and below that, the reasons why we *shouldn't*.
After Carolann and Malcolm add their ideas
and their comments, the list looks like this:

SHOULD

1. We can find out for sure what all this stuff really is and how much it's worth.

> True—I can't tell a ruby from a piece of glass painted with red nail polish.

2. We don't have to hide anything anymore.

> **Yeah, I'm tired of sneaking around. But then—will we have to hide ourselves from the papers if we get famous?**

3. We might be rich, even if we don't get to keep everything.

> This could be one reason our folks won't be so mad once they know what we've been doing.

> **I wouldn't mind finding out what it's like to have extra money. Plus we could do some good things for people if we get rich.**

4. We can finally get some sleep.

> **Amen!**

> Ditto. I think I could sleep for a whole week.

SHOULDN'T

1. Once we hand over our treasure, then what? Do we have rights?

> Good point. Harry says he knows this Trent guy pretty well—but still . . . how will we feel when he takes it back to his lab?
>
> **Right. . . . Can we still see it? Will we get the credit? Will we get any of the money?**

2. This whole thing might be illegal. We could get arrested or something.

> **<u>Maybe</u>—but wouldn't Harry have told us that already?**
>
> I doubt it. I mean, people dive down in the ocean to look for treasure all the time. We just dug ours up.

3. We're not adults, so maybe they'll say our parents get to decide what happens with all the stuff in the chest.

> **Yeah, I thought of this, too. But let's say we keep it—now Harry and this Trent guy know about it—we'd have to hide it somewhere else till we're 21. I don't want to wait that long.**
>
> Or we'd need to sell it secretly (to who? and for how much?).

We talk about each point on the list.
We   weigh   every   possibility.
Then we vote.

TECHNICALLY...

A few days after we turn our treasure over
to Trent Taylor and his lab workers,
Malcolm and me are watching TV when our

new lawyer (the professor said we should get one)
calls: "Because the chest was found on the A.M.E. grounds,
it technically belongs to the church," he explains.

"In order to claim the contents, the church
would need to assign ownership of the treasure to you."
I almost faint again. How could we have done

all that thinking, all that sneaking and digging—
all that work—and not be the legal owners?
As I'm thinking these depressing thoughts, Malcolm

bolts for the street, leaps onto his bike, and pedals
off. A half hour later, the phone rings. "Get Carolann
and meet me at the church, soon as you can. . . ."

WHO'S REALLY IN CHARGE?

We arrive just before five, in time
to see Malcolm's aunt Eunice—
dressed in what looks like her Sunday suit
and carrying a Bible under her right arm—
enter the front door of the A.M.E. Church.
Malcolm heads us off at the steps. "My
dad's inside with the elders," he tells us.
"And I just finished explaining everything,
including our legal situation, to my aunt.
Now *she's* gonna try to convince them
to sign the rights to the chest over to us."
With her gum, Carolann blows a giant bubble.
"Sooo . . . what do *we* do?" she inquires.
Malcolm shrugs. "We wait right here
in case they want to talk to us," he replies.
Carolann sighs. "I seem to be spending
a lot of my free time on these steps."
I ask Malcolm: "How serious do you think
the elders will take your aunt Eunice?"
Malcolm rolls his eyes. "My dad might
be the pastor . . . but his sister *runs*
the place. If anyone can get them to
sign, it's my aunt." I sit down between
Carolann and Malcolm and take out
my kaleidoscope. We pass it back
and forth, each taking a turn at
looking through the lens,

at a hundred little glass pieces
that spin and glitter like uncut gems.

JUDGMENT DAY

We stand to the side
as the Willowbank A.M.E. elders file silently by.
A few of them nod, smile.
Finally, Aunt Eunice appears, her Bible tucked
under her right arm, her pink hat tilted back, her forehead
speckled with sweat. She hands Malcolm a letter
signed by all the elders,
giving us exclusive rights to the treasure.

"Luke 12:13–21, the Parable of the Rich Fool . . .
one of my favorites," she explains, nodding toward the
half-dozen men and women walking across the parking lot.
"I reminded our elders that *we* did not
find those maps,
     locate that chest,
          dig and dig until our hands bled
               and we were short of sleep."

She pauses, mops her brow with a handkerchief.
"I reminded them that *we* did not
plan and worry and weep
over how to honor a grandfather's last dream,
or agonize over how and when to ask someone for help:
'The Lord did not lead any of *us* to that spot,' I told them.
'The Lord saw fit to lead *those three kids*
to a place in our woods
where He showed them a hidden treasure . . .
and, Brothers and Sisters, He will *not* be pleased
if we reap the wheat that we have not sown,
if we keep the riches that we do not morally own.' "

Maybe I've just spent too many years around Denise,
but I admit I'm always shocked when people
do the right thing, when doing the wrong thing
would be so much easier.
"Thanks, Aunt Eunice," I manage to croak,
which seems like a too-little word, considering
what she just did for us.

She lifts the arm that isn't holding the Bible, wraps it
around the backs of all three of us—and squeezes.
"You know . . . ," she whispers, "we pray every Sunday
that the Lord will provide our church
with a new roof. . . ."
She gives us one last squeeze
and Malcolm a big, wet kiss on the cheek
before she leaves.

Malcolm, smiling sheepishly, wipes his face with his sleeve.

Carolann squeals: "Malcolm, you *are* a genius!"

"Like I told you," he says, handing me the signed letter. "She runs the place!"

Part 10

Somebody calls you, you answer quite slowly,
A girl with kaleidoscope eyes.

—from "Lucy in the Sky with Diamonds"
by John Lennon and Paul McCartney

TWO WEEKS INTO SCHOOL

and we are already missing summer.
Once the word spread around town
about our finding a pirate treasure,
we became almost like
celebrities, except with chores and homework.

I thought, with all the press
and even a quick mention of us
on CBS,
that maybe—just maybe—I'd hear
from Mom.

But so far, nothing.
As Grandma used to say whenever Gramps promised
to spend weekends
painting the house and the porch
instead of staying in the attic with his maps:
"I'm not holding my breath."

But anyway, it's Saturday, and phone calls,
fan mail, and homework

will have to wait.
I grab half an English muffin from the pantry,
stop for a quick look in the hallway mirror.
With my new haircut, my nice blouse,
and Denise's old peasant skirt,
I could pass for a college kid myself.

Malcolm's already outside; Carolann's walking across
the street. They are both dressed up nice.
When Dad pulls our car around,
we pile into the backseat and drive off, waving to
the twins, who are hanging off the Motts' front porch,
wearing their new pirate costumes, a patch over
their two left eyes.

ANOTHER ROAD TRIP

The sun's warm for September but there
is already a crispness in the air.
"Perfect sailing weather," Gramps would say.

On our way north to the interstate,
we pass a lot of folks heading south,
going to the shore for maybe the last time this year.

It's funny how, since the treasure took up
all my energy this summer,
I didn't have time to be envious
like I always used to be. Now I'm looking through the windows,
wishing the passengers a safe trip
to Wildwood, Avalon, or Stone Harbor.

I smooth my skirt, settle back in the seat
of Dad's station wagon, and listen
to the news on WOR. When they start
to give the war report,
Dad glances into the rearview mirror
at Malcolm, who's reading another letter from Dixon.
"That's OK, Mr. Bradley," Malcolm says
as Dad reaches for the tuner. "I'm used to it by now."
And then to me: "Dixon's platoon captain
made him a scout. Do you think that's
a good thing?"

I try to imagine Dixon creeping through the jungle
in a helmet and camouflage,
checking for signs of the enemy
while the rest of his platoon waits for word
of what's ahead. I don't think it's such a
good thing—but what can I say?

"Well . . ." I hesitate. "They probably really
depend on him . . . ," I continue, trying to sound
as positive as I can. "So they probably give him

the best food and more rest
and plenty of ammunition."
I glance to see if my answer satisfies Malcolm.
I can't tell. He's reading the letter
over and over again, and then—
I don't know why—
I have to turn and look out the window.
I bite my lower lip. *Jeez, Lyza—don't cry.*

Meanwhile, Carolann jabbers on about
some of the new kids at school—
where they moved from, what they say or play or own.
(She's convinced one of the ninth graders
is in the Witness Protection Program:
"He forgot his *name* the other day," she explains.)

The drive takes a little more
than an hour. We make a quick stop
to pick up Harry Keating, who's been staying
at a hotel near the Princeton campus
and working with our new lawyer, Mr. Jarvis,
on the legal details
so we can stay home and start school.

Dad turns off Nassau Street,
steers us through the granite gates of the university,
beneath the canopy of ancient maples,
between old stone buildings
with Gothic arches and neat brick sidewalks,

until we reach the one with the sign
we've seen in all the newspaper photos:
MCCORMICK HALL, DEPT. OF ART & ARCHAEOLOGY.

IVY LEAGUE

Professor Taylor greets us and leads us
to his office on the second floor. Our

lawyer is there and he speaks for a few
minutes with Harry, then with my father.

Dad smiles over at me once. I think
he's still confused about all of this,

but somehow he also seems relieved.
I guess there was a part of him

that thought I was heading for trouble,
spinning into some kind of delinquency

from which I would never return. The truth
about what I've been doing all summer,

though strange in its own way, is a lot better
than what he'd been afraid of. Professor

Taylor leaves them, motions for us to
follow him down the long, dark hall

posted with neat red arrows that say:
ARCHAEOLOGY LAB—EMPLOYEES ONLY.

ON DISPLAY

Opening the padlocked doors, he takes us
into a separate room with rows of
                              low tables
and special lamps hanging from the ceiling.
It's dark, but we can see the walls,
which are lined with shelves, filled with boxes,
beakers, and bags,
all carefully labeled and tagged
with the numbers and names of excavation sites:
    Santa Fe, New Mexico;
    St. Louis, Missouri;
    Bismarck, North Dakota;
    Williamsburg, Virginia.

We follow Professor Taylor to the back,
to the very last table, which is covered with
a piece of black plastic. He asks us to stand beside it
while he pulls the plastic off.
He flicks on a switch.
The lamp hanging from the ceiling spotlights
the neatly typed label in the center:

> Site 164, Bradley, Mott, Dupree;
> Willowbank, NJ; August 1968.

There are framed newspaper clippings and photographs
of the three of us standing next to
the chest
just as Professor Taylor and his team of archaeologists
are lifting it carefully—oh so carefully—
with a special set of pulleys (not too different from the one
Malcolm drew that night on a napkin in the diner)
from the hole.
I get goose bumps again just remembering that day—
we taped interviews for several TV stations,
and the *New York Times* even sent a reporter
down to meet us.
"Teens Dig Up Riches in South Jersey Churchyard,"
the headline said.

Professor Taylor adjusts the light so we can see
the whole display:

the contents of the treasure chest
cleaned up, labeled, and laid out across the long lab table.

Almost everything is there:
    the two big gems;
    the English gold, the Spanish silver;
    the jeweled necklaces and rings;
    the small metal box that held the strange white powder
        (which is opium, as it turns out; used as medicine
        at sea, then sold if the crew made it home safely);
    the few pieces of mostly disintegrated cloth, now sealed
        in plastic and marked *silk*, *linen*, or *cotton*;
    and finally the two bezoar stones, which the captain kept
        as an antidote for poison (too bad they didn't prevent hanging).

"Far out!" Carolann squeals.

"I wish Dixon could see this," Malcolm whispers.

"Gramps, too," I add.

"I'll be in the next room if you need me,"
the professor says. "I'll give you three
some time to enjoy this privately—
then I'll come and close up."

For the next half hour or so,
we walk around and around that table,
pointing and looking, laughing and joking,

reliving all the nights we spent searching—
then digging, digging, digging—
remembering all the planning and worrying,
all the hard decisions.

Now, looking back after all of that, it feels like
the whole summer went past in a flash.
And here we are: three local kids who followed
some maps left in an attic
and found a real pirate treasure.
"You've given our office a real lift," one reporter said
after she interviewed us. "We've had so much bad news
coming in from the war,
it's high time we reported something *happy* like this!"
I considered telling her that we still think about
the war, about Dixon and other guys like him, every day.
But she was so clearly enjoying our story . . .
I didn't.

OMISSION

After we leave the lab, I think about
the spyglass,
hidden at home under the winter sweaters
tucked beneath my bed: the one that,
when I held it up and looked through my window,
let me see over all the roofs in town
and down along the Mullica River
and up the hill, almost to Gramps' grave;
the one with the initials of William Kidd,
the one my two best friends know I have,
the one Professor Taylor and his team of archaeologists
must have surely figured out
made the indentation in the half-disintegrated linen
they found in the chest . . . the one
no one, so far, has asked me about.

ONE FINAL LITTLE DETAIL

Before we go back to Willowbank,
the professor asks us to wait in the next room
while he speaks alone
with Harry.

The day after we first met Trent Taylor,
we voted to make Harry
the "executor" of our treasure,
and he's been overseeing   everything
that the university's been doing
since we gave them permission to excavate the chest
and to study and catalog
every object in it.

Harry—who's still Hairy, but seems a lot more
grown-up and reliable than before—
has been calling us almost every day,
telling us which museums have inquired about
buying the coins and gems, telling us what
Professor Taylor and his team have discovered
about the objects: where they came from,
how much they could be worth,
and how Captain Kidd
might have come to have them
in his chest.

Harry even got us Mr. Jarvis, whose specialty
is watching out for people
who have won gameshows
or who suddenly have a lot of money for some reason
and need protection from all the schemers
and other greedy sorts
who might try to take advantage of three
South Jersey teens who just happened to make
history
in the backyard of a church.

Five minutes later, the office door opens.
Harry steps out, walks across
to where we are standing by the window,
watching the Princeton kids filing out of class.
He hands me a piece of paper
folded in half.
"That number is the total projected value of your treasure.
Divide by three and that's—"

"FOUR!" I remind him. "We wouldn't have
finished this if you hadn't—"

"Forget it, Lyza," Harry interrupts.
"This has been more interesting than
anything I've ever done." He nods toward
his professor-friend. "I might have a job here next year,
as Trent's lab assistant. That wouldn't
have happened if you hadn't trusted me."

Jeez. Harry Keating working at Princeton!
(Dad perks up at this news. I picture Denise's Janis Joplin
poster in one of the nice houses we saw
on the way over here.)

I look down at the paper folded in my hands.
"*Wait!*" Carolann commands.
She takes my arm, leads me to an
overstuffed chair. "Sit there . . . your new habit
of losing consciousness makes me nervous!"

She sits on one arm of the chair, Malcolm
stands beside the other. I flip up
the top of the folded paper so that the three of us
can read the number together:

    12 . . . followed by six zeros.

And this time, I do not faint.

TRUST

We're only thirteen and that means
we're legally minors, so even though our treasure
is worth a LOT,
our lawyer, our parents, Harry, and Professor Taylor
will help us decide if and when
we put the treasure up for auction
or if we sell it to museums, and then
we have to keep the money in a trust fund
till we turn twenty-one.

In the meantime, our parents are *very* happy.
Well, OK. *Carolann's parents* are very happy:
    They're together and they don't fight.
    They don't have a son in Vietnam.
    They're setting up a college fund for Carolann.

Mr. Mott came over after dinner last night
to visit with Dad and to watch
the Phillies play the Pittsburgh Pirates.
Carolann came, too,
and showed me the book she's reading:
Pearson's Guide to Starting Your Own Detective Agency.
"It's still what I want to do," she told me.
"Now I'll just have nicer office furniture
and a larger sign—and maybe an assistant or two."

As for Malcolm's parents,
they're as happy as they *can* be, given all the depressing headlines

they read about the casualties in Vietnam.
(Two more guys from Willowbank came home
in flag-draped coffins last week.
Another neighbor, Alex Palmer, who lives just down the street,
came back with no legs. All day, every day,
he sits in his wheelchair on the porch.)
I think we could have dug up a treasure worth
a billion dollars
and if it didn't bring Dixon back home safe,
the Duprees would just ignore it.

Still, when we stopped in on our way
back from Princeton, Mrs. Dupree hugged me
about twenty-five times. She cut me a big piece
of lemon cake and made me sit
down in their kitchen to explain *again*
how I found the maps, how we—all together—
located the treasure, how we dug it up as much
as we could before we told anyone else.
"Your gramps would be real proud of you, Lyza."
And to Malcolm: "I guess that explains
why I was always finding dirt clods in your pockets!"
But she hugged him, too, and you could tell
she was proud of what he'd done,
even though he did have to sneak out a lot.

Mr. Dupree says any money that comes to them
he'll use for a new church roof
and keep the rest for Malcolm's and Dixon's futures.

As for my dad, he *does* seem happier than before.
He's actually talking about taking
a sabbatical
and fixing up our house.
All along I thought he was working so much
to avoid being with us—
but really he was just trying to pay off
the debt Mom left.
I remember how Gramps used to say:
"Lyza, there's two sides to a coin, two sides to a ship,
and two sides to every story,"
and though I never quite understood how
that could be true for a *family*, I see now
that he was absolutely right.

DOWNTOWN

Tonight, for a change, we cook dinner together:
Dad makes macaroni and cheese, I make
corn bread, Denise burns the peas.

After we eat and Denise leaves for work, Dad and I take a walk.
I know he's still trying to figure out why
his own father left those maps to me
and not to him. "I always thought he trusted me," Dad says.

I try to explain: "He did, Dad. But, no offense . . .
you are so predictable,
and you thought his adventures were foolish.
Gramps knew if he left you his maps
and those numbers and that key,
you might never have even bothered
to go to Brigantine."

Dad waves to Mr. Reece at the end of our street,
who's letting his four kids
dance through the fountain of his garden hose.
In the next house, Alex Palmer rolls
back and forth across the porch,
his wheelchair squealing.
"You're probably right," Dad says at last.
"I don't know if I would've taken the time
to do much about them.
To tell you the truth, I haven't had the energy for anything
besides teaching these past two years. . . ."

His voice trails off as we walk a couple more blocks,
turn the corner by the diner. We can see a few
of the waitresses and a busboy,
and after a minute or two
we see Denise waiting on a couple
seated in a window booth.

We stop on the sidewalk,
wave our hands over our heads.

She sees us and waves back, and in that minute
she looks just like Mom.
Dad keeps waving even after she turns again
to her customers.

I walk ahead a little to give him time.
He catches up, puts his arm through mine,
and we walk like that for a while.

Finally, he speaks: "So I guess now that you've found
the chest, you won't be sneaking around so much . . .
and I guess this also means you're really
not taking any drugs."

I give him my annoyed sideways look.
He holds up his hand, grinning: "I'm kidding, I'm kidding!!"

He sighs, runs his fingers through his hair.
"I'm sorry about all that, Lyza. But I thought, you know . . .
the way you've had to be on your own
so much . . . with your mother gone
and me teaching all the time—everything is so *crazy* these days."

His voice drifts off and is lost in the noise
of passing traffic on Main Street.
We buy two orange Creamsicles and sit
on the bench before Miller's grocery store,
watching the sun set behind the line of cars
filled with families

coming back from the beach, looking tired
but mostly, happy.

VISUAL AID

Dear Dixon,

We are all doing fine here in Willowbank. By
now Malcolm's probably told you about our
pretty weird summer, about what we found in
the churchyard and all the rest. He says you're a
scout now—I guess that's a pretty important
job. So I am sending something with this letter
to help you see what's ahead. It's old, but it still
works pretty good. Don't worry if you lose it—
it's been lost before and I'm sure someone else
will find it and put it to good use. Be careful out
there. We look forward to when you come
home.

Your friend,
Lyza B.

P.S. Denise sends her good karma. Harry says,
"Hang in there, man!"

VISIT

On my way back from mailing the spyglass
to Dixon,
I make a stop at Gramps' grave. I tear away
a few of the weeds
that have grown up either side of the stone.
I sit next to him awhile,
telling him everything that's happened to me
this summer, even though
I believe somehow he already knows.

Afterward, I walk to the A.M.E. Church, where
the choir is practicing
for Sunday and their hearty hallelujahs spill
from the open windows
and float out over the yard where we spent
so many late
summer hours. I slip into the back, kneel down,
and just like I
promised I would, I say a prayer for Janis Joplin
—and Denise.

AND LATER...

I take my kaleidoscope off the shelf,
look through the little hole at the end
of the cardboard tube;

I turn   and turn   and turn   and turn,

letting the crystals shift into strange
and beautiful patterns, letting the pieces fall
wherever they will.

AUTHOR'S NOTE

Although this is primarily a work of fiction, the following is a list of places and people in the story that were drawn from real life:

Willowbank, New Jersey: This fictional town is a composite of the many small South Jersey boroughs that, as a child, I remember passing through on our family's annual pilgrimage to the shore. Today, many of them still experience a several-mile backlog of weekend traffic as tens of thousands of visitors make their way to the beach from New York and Philadelphia.

Tuckahoe, New Jersey: This actual South Jersey town lies about ten miles northwest of Ocean City, New Jersey. It has a rich history dating from the time of the Lenape Indians, who named it for one of their favored foods, a breadlike vegetable substance that they found at the base of trees (see www.tuckahoenj.com/history.html).

Brigantine, New Jersey: Formerly known as East Atlantic City, Brigantine lies several miles northeast of Atlantic City on its own island. Its lighthouse, which was built to attract tourists, is well known as a New Jersey Shore landmark. The Brigantine Beach Historical Museum & Society established in 1992 provides a wonderful Web site (see bibliography) and information on the town's history, including pirate anecdotes and legends. The scenes that take place in the Brigantine Historical Society in this book, however, are largely fictional and are based on my visits to various archives, libraries, and historical societies in the course of my research for biographies and novels.

Mullica River: If you look at a New Jersey map, you will discover this river flowing southeastward across the lower portion of the state before emptying into the Great Bay, just north of Atlantic City. The Mullica's tributaries include about two dozen smaller creeks, which join it throughout thousands of acres of rich wetlands. The river provides drainage for the extensive Pinelands region of southern New Jersey, is easy to navigate, and remains popular today with fishermen, kayakers, and canoeists.

In this story, however, I was inspired by an incident that occurred in the mid-1800s on the Missouri River, which I'd first read about in *Smithsonian* magazine (December 2006). The article described how, in 1987 and 1988, a father and son located and excavated a steamship loaded with valuable cargo, which they believed had sunk in 1856 after hitting a submerged tree. Over the years, as the Missouri River shifted course, the steamship *Arabia* became buried under a Kansas cornfield (see the bibliography for more on this). I became fascinated with the idea of buried treasure and shifting rivers and incorporated both of these motifs into *Kaleidoscope Eyes*.

Princeton, New Jersey, and Princeton University: This lovely, history-rich town and its outstanding university do, of course, exist, and McCormick Hall currently houses the Art & Archaeology Department. Professor Trent Taylor and the scenes in this story that take place at Princeton are fictional, however.

Janis Joplin: Born and raised in Port Arthur, Texas, Janis Joplin rose to fame as a singer-songwriter in the early 1960s. As the lead singer of the blues-rock group Big Brother and the Holding Company, Janis performed in concert halls and at music festivals across the country from 1963 to 1970. Like her songs, Janis was intense and rebellious, qualities that endeared her to her fans and made her an entertainment icon of the sixties. Sadly, Janis developed a serious drug and alcohol problem, which she couldn't overcome. She died of a heroin overdose in 1970, at age twenty-seven.

Captain William Kidd: The main biographical information in this story regarding the captain is accurate. Kidd began his career as a respectable ship's captain, then became a privateer (commander of a private warship sent out by the government to attack enemy vessels) and finally a somewhat reluctant pirate who had hopes of returning to his quiet family life after several years of plundering. While I found no evidence that he ever sailed up the Mullica River with his first mate and a treasure chest (see above under "Mullica River"), there is a legend that he buried treasure along the East Coast. According to the Brigantine Beach Historical Museum & Society, Kidd *did* come ashore there (about twenty-five miles from the treasure in this story) to bury treasure in the late 1690s, and he is reputed to have killed his first mate, Timothy Jones, after doing so. That treasure has never been found. Because pirates were secretive, most left little or no written record of their various journeys and activities. The ship's-log entries in my story are therefore fictional, even though the historical facts of Kidd's life are not.

An amazing discovery was made about Captain Kidd while I was writing this book. In December 2007, the wreck of Kidd's ship the *Quedagh Merchant* was discovered in shallow water off the island of Catalina in the Dominican Republic. It appears that Kidd left the *Merchant,* which he and his crew had stolen from a powerful nobleman off the coast of India, in the care of his crew in the Caribbean and took a lighter, faster ship up the east coast of America (which was still in its colonial period) to try to clear his name and return to his family.

As of 2009, the wreck is being explored, its contents protected and inventoried. For further information, go to www.sciencedaily.com/releases/2007/12/071213162036.htm.

FOR FURTHER READING

About Captain William Kidd, Pirates, and Buried Treasure:

Bordewich, Fergus M. "Pay Dirt." *Smithsonian,* December 2006.

Garwood, Val. *The World of the Pirate.* New York: Peter Bedrick Books, 1997.

Hawley, Greg. *Treasure in a Cornfield: The Discovery and Excavation of the Steamship* Arabia. Kansas City, MO: Paddle Wheel Publishing, 1998.

Platt, Richard. *Pirate* (Eyewitness Books series). London: DK Publishing, 1994.

Zacks, Richard. *The Pirate Hunter: The True Story of Captain Kidd.* New York: Hyperion, 2002.

www.brigantinebeachnj.com/history_pirates.html

www.historic-uk.com/HistoryUK/Scotland-History/CaptainKidd.htm

www.nationalgeographic.com/pirates

www.piratemuseum.com/pirate.html

www.pirates-of-nassau.com/home.htm

About the Vietnam War:

Clinton, Catherine. *The Black Soldier: 1492 to the Present.* Boston: Houghton Mifflin, 2000.

Edelman, Bernard, ed. *Dear America: Letters Home from Vietnam.* New York: W. W. Norton & Co., 1985.

Isserman, Maurice. *Vietnam War*. New York: Facts on File, 2003.

The Vietnam War with Walter Cronkite (DVD). Marathon Music & Video, 2003.

www.english.uiuc.edu/maps/vietnam/antiwar.html

www.oakton.edu/user/~wittman/chronol.htm

About 1968 and the 1960s Culture and Music:

Holland, Gini. *A Cultural History of the United States Through the Decades: The 1960s*. San Diego: Lucent Books, 1998.

McWilliams, John C. *The 1960s Cultural Revolution*. Westport, CT: Greenwood Press, 2000.

The Sixties: The Years That Shaped a Generation (DVD). PBS Home Video, 2005.

This Fabulous Century: 1960–1970. Time-Life Books, 1970.

www.officialjanis.com

www.rockhall.com/inductee/janis-joplin

www.stg.brown.edu/projects/1968

ACKNOWLEDGMENTS

I am deeply grateful to the following individuals for their guidance, support, and expertise:

Joan Slattery, senior executive editor at Knopf, and Allison Wortche, assistant editor at Knopf, whose keen sense of structure and scene helped me to shape the many threads of this story into a single historical mystery; Fergus M. Bordewich, whose wonderful article "Pay Dirt," which I first read in the December 2006 issue of *Smithsonian* magazine, piqued my interest in modern treasure hunting; and Richard Zacks, whose meticulously researched and most entertaining book *The Pirate Hunter: The True Story of Captain Kidd* provided me with a thorough understanding of the life and times of the infamous sailor. And also to the following for their patient and generous assistance in clarifying the rules concerning museum acquisitions and abandoned-property rights: Greg Landrey, fellow Gettysburg College alumnus and Director of the Library, Collections Management, and Academic Programs at Winterthur Museum & Country Estate in Delaware; Beth Parker Miller and Onie Rollins, also of Winterthur; Mark Falzini, Archivist at the New Jersey State Police Museum & Learning Center; and Tim Decker, Collections Manager, New Jersey Historical Society. Maddy Oberholtzer's artistic eye and Diane Gies' research expertise were also very helpful. And finally, thanks to my husband, Neil, and to my daughter, Leigh, for putting up with my scattered rough drafts, my notes scribbled on napkins, my many piles of books, and my quirky imagination. I couldn't do this job without you.